Butterflies in November

'Charmingly done... funny and wistful, but there's a darker narrative just beneath the surface... What begins as a tragicomic, quirky tale develops into a very moving, layered and optimistic piece of writing'   *FT*

'With subtle prose and sardonic humor Ólafsdóttir upends expectations'   *New York Times*

'Evocative, humorous... The beguiling imagery captures the fragile and fleeting beauty of those loved and lost, as well as the possibilities of self reinvention; of shedding skins, growing wings'   *Observer*

'Sadness and humour coexist beautifully in *Butterflies in November*'
Metro

'The author... takes mundane subjects in life... and makes them quirky, fun, adorable and bizarre. You'll savour each page of this book'   *Company*

'Gorgeously quirky'   *Stylist*

'[*Butterflies in November*] has many bleak moments, but plenty of funny ones too... we warm to Ólafsdóttir's clear-eyed, quirky heroine'   *Daily Mail*

HOTEL SILENCE

Auður Ava Ólafsdóttir

Translated from the Icelandic
by Brian FitzGibbon

PUSHKIN PRESS

Pushkin Press
71–75 Shelton Street
London, WC2H 9JQ

Original text © 2016 by Auður Ava Ólafsdóttir
English translation © 2018 by Brian FitzGibbon
Hotel Silence was first published as *Ör* in Iceland, 2016
First published by Pushkin Press in 2018

Excerpt from "For My Lover, Returning to His Wife" from *The Complete Poems of Anne Sexton*. Copyright © 1967, 1968, 1969 by Anne Sexton. Reprinted by permission of the Estate of Anne Sexton; excerpt from "Football Season is Over" by Hunter S. Thompson used by the permission of the Gonzo Trust; excerpts from "One Art" by Elizabeth Bishop, from *Poems by Elizabeth Bishop* published by Chatto & Windus. Reproduced by permission of The Random House Group Ltd. © 2011

We thank the Icelandic Literature Center for their generous financial support of this translation.

ICELANDIC LITERATURE CENTER

10 9 8 7 6 5 4 3 2 1

ISBN 13: 978-1-78227-421-6

Published by arrangement with Éditions Zulma, Paris

Typeset by Tetragon, London
Printed and bound by CPI Group (UK) Ltd, Croydon CRO 4YY

www.pushkinpress.com

Dedicated to all the unknown victims: nurses, teachers, bartenders, poets, schoolchildren, librarians, and electricians.

And also to J.

The formation of a scar is a natural part of the biological process, which occurs when a lesion to the skin or other body tissue grows after an accident, illness, or surgery. Since the body is unable to create an exact replica of the damaged tissue, the fresh tissue grows with a new texture and properties that differ from the undamaged skin around it.

The navel is our centre or core and by that we mean the centre of the universe. It is a scar that no longer serves a purpose.

—Bland.is

CONTENTS

HOTEL
SILENCE

31 MAY

I know how ludicrous I look naked, nevertheless I start to undress, first my trousers and socks, then I unbutton my shirt, revealing the glistening white water lily on my pink flesh, half a knife's length away from the muscular organ that pumps eight thousand litres of blood a day, finally I take off my underpants—all in that order. It doesn't take long. Then I stand stark naked on the parquet floor in front of the woman, I am as God made me, plus forty-nine years and four days, not that my thoughts are on God at this moment. We are still separated by three floorboards, massive pinewood from the surrounding forest, which is carpeted with mines, each floorboard is thirty centimetres wide, with intermittent gaps, and I stretch out my arms, groping towards her like a blind man trying to catch his bearings. First I reach the surface of the body, the skin, a streak of moonlight caressing her back through a slit between the curtains. She takes one step towards me, I step on a creaking floorboard. And she also holds out her hand, measuring palm against palm, lifeline against lifeline, and I feel a turbulence gushing through my carotid artery and also a pulsation in my knees and arms, how the blood flows from organ to organ. Leaf-patterned wallpaper adorns the walls around the bed in room eleven of Hotel Silence and I think to myself, tomorrow I'll start to sandpaper and polish the floor.

I

FLESH

The skin is the largest organ of the human body. The skin of a fully grown adult has a surface area of two square metres and weighs five kilos. In many other animals the skin is referred to as the hide or pelt. In old Icelandic the word skin also means flesh.

5 MAY

The table in Tryggvi's Tattoo Parlour is covered with small glass jars of multicoloured inks and the young man asks me if I've chosen a picture yet or whether I'm thinking of a personal pattern or symbol?

He himself is covered in tattoos all over his body. I observe a snake winding up his neck and wrapping itself around a black skull. Ink flows through his limbs and the triceps of the arm that holds the needle sports a coil of triple barbed wire.

"Many people come here to camouflage their scars," says the tattooist, talking to me in the mirror. When he turns around, as far as I can make out, the hooves of a prancing horse emerge from the back of his vest.

He bends over a stack of plastic folders, chooses one, and runs his eyes over it to find a picture to show me.

"Wings are a big favourite among middle-aged men," I hear him say, and then notice that there are four swords piercing a flaming heart on his other upper arm.

I have a total of seven scars on my body, four above my belly button, the point of origin, and three below it. A bird wing that would cover the shoulder, say from the neck down to the collarbone, would conceal two, even three of them.

Like a familiar and comforting old acquaintance, its wing could become the feathered shadow of myself, my shield and fortress. The oily plumage would mantle the exposed vulnerable pink flesh.

The kid flips swiftly through drawings to show me various versions of bird wings, finally pointing his index finger at one image:

"Eagle wings are the most popular."

He could have added, what man doesn't dream of being a bird of prey, drifting solitarily across the globe, soaring over mountain lagoons, gullies, and marshes, hunting for a prey to snatch?

But instead he says:

"Just take your time."

And he explains to me that he has another customer in a chair on the other side of the curtain and that he is just about to finish the national flag, complete with flapping and shading.

He lowers his voice.

"I told him the flagpole would bend if he put on two kilos but he insisted on having it."

I was planning on dropping in on Mom before her nap and wanted to wind this transaction up as quickly as possible.

"I was thinking of a drill."

If my request has taken him by surprise, he shows no sign of it and immediately starts searching through the appropriate folder.

"We might have a drill in here somewhere under domestic appliances," he says. "Anyway, it's no more complicated than the quad bike I did last week."

"No, I was joking," I say.

He looks at me with a grave air and it's difficult to decipher whether he's offended or not.

I hurriedly dig into my pocket and pull out a folded sheet of paper, open the drawing, and hand it to him. He takes it and irons out all the corners before finally holding it up to the light. I've managed to surprise him. He is unable to conceal his incertitude.

"Is this a flower or . . ."

"A water lily," I say without hesitation.

"And just one colour?"

"Yes, just one colour, white. No shadowing," I add.

"And no inscription?"

"No, no inscription."

He puts the folders back, says he can do the flower freehand, and turns on the tattoo drill.

"And where do you want it?"

He prepares to dip the needle into a white liquid.

I unbutton my shirt and point at my heart.

"We'll have to shave the hair first," he says, turning off the drill. "Otherwise your flower will be lost in the darkness of a forest."

I mention the state where the slow suicide
of all men goes under the name of "life"

The shortest route to the old folk's home is through the graveyard.

I've always imagined that the fifth month would be the last month of my life and that there would be more than one five in that final date, if not the fifth of the fifth, then the fifteenth of the fifth or the twenty-fifth of the fifth. That would also be the month of my birthday. The ducks would have completed their mating by then, but there wouldn't just be ducks on the lake but also oystercatchers and purple sandpipers, because there would be birdsong on the nightless spring day I cease to exist.

Will the world miss me? No. Will the world be any poorer without me? No. Will the world survive without me? Yes. Is the world a better place now than when I came into it? No. What have I done to improve it? Nothing.

On my way down Skothúsvegur I reflect on how one should go about borrowing a hunting rifle from a neighbour. Does one borrow a weapon the same way one borrows a hose extension? What animals are hunted at the beginning of May? One can't shoot the messenger of spring, the golden plover, who has just returned to the island, or a duck hatching from an egg. Could I say that I want to shoot a great black-backed gull that keeps me awake in the attic apartment of a residential block in the city centre? Wouldn't

Svanur find it suspicious if I were to suddenly turn into a spokesman for ducklings' rights? Besides, Svanur knows that I'm no hunter. Although I've experienced standing in the middle of a freezing cold river in my crotch-high boots, alone up on a heath, and felt the cold pressing against my body like a thick wall and pebbles on the spongy bed under my waders, and then felt how the river swiftly tugged at me below, how the bottom deepened and vanished, while I stared into the gaping, sucking vortex, I have never fired a gun. On my last fishing trip I came home with two trout, which I filleted and fried with chives I trimmed off a pot on the balcony. Svanur also knows that I can't bear violence after he tried to drag me to see *Die Hard 4*. What does one shoot in May apart from one's self? Or a fellow Homo sapiens? He would put two and two together.

Svanur isn't the kind of man who asks questions, though. Or who generally contemplates one's inner life. He isn't the kind of guy who would mention a full moon or comment on the northern lights. He'd never speak of *the rainbow colours at the outermost ends of human knowledge*. He wouldn't even point out the colours in the sky to his wife, Aurora, the rose-pink hue of daybreak, he wouldn't say, "There she is, your namesake." No more than Aurora would mention the sky to her husband. There's a clear division of tasks in their household and she alone drags the teenager out of bed in the morning. He, on the other hand, takes care of walking their fourteen-year-old border collie bitch who hobbles lamely in the front. No, Svanur wouldn't mix any feelings into the issue, he'd just hand me the rifle and say, that's a Remington 40-XB, bedded but with the original lock and barrel, even if he suspected I was going to shoot myself.

> The navel is a scar on people's abdomen, which formed when the remains of the umbilical cord dropped off. When a child is born, the umbilical cord is clamped and then cut to sever the link between mother and child. The first scar is therefore connected to the mother

The old folks sit stooped on park benches under woollen blankets in the cold spring sun, with a flock of geese nearby, paired off in twos. I notice a bird huddled on its own apart from the group, and it doesn't move, even when I walk up to it. One of its wings is bent backwards, clearly broken. The wounded goose is partnerless and won't procreate. God is sending me a message. Not that I believe in him.

My mother slouches in a recliner, her feet don't touch the ground, her slippers are too big, above them are her twiggy legs, she's shrivelled to almost nothing, she has ceased to be flesh, as light as a feather, held together by her Styrofoam bones and a few tendons. What comes to mind is the weathered skeleton of a bird that has been left on the heath all winter; the vacant carcass remains, but ultimately disintegrates, turning into a ball of dust with claws. It is hard to imagine that this scrawny little woman, who doesn't reach my shoulders, once inhabited a female form. I recognise her special-occasion skirt, which has grown far too baggy around the waist, far too big on her, clothes that belong to a former life, another time zone.

I'm not going to end up like Mom.

A smell hangs in the air, I walk through clouds of vapour emanating from bulging meatballs and cabbage. On the food cart in the corridor there are plastic bowls half full of red cabbage and rhubarb jam. Cutlery noises blend with the utterances of the personnel who alternately raise and deepen their voices to make themselves heard by their charges. There isn't space for much furniture in the room, apart from an organ pushed up against a wall; the former maths teacher and organ player was allowed to keep it with her, once it seemed certain that she would never play it again.

Beside the bed there are bookshelves that bear witness to my mother's hobby: world wars, not least World War II. There's Napoleon Bonaparte and Attila the Hun standing side by side, and a book about the Korean War and another about Vietnam sandwiched between two leather-bound volumes marked *World War I* and *World War II* in Danish.

My visits are subject to daily rituals that are chiselled in stone and the first thing she asks me is if I've washed my hands.

"Did you wash your hands?"

"I did."

"It isn't enough to just rinse them, you've got to hold them under the hot tap for thirty seconds."

It suddenly occurs to me that I was once inside her.

I'm one metre eighty-five centimetres tall and the last time I stepped onto a scale—in the locker room of a swimming pool—I weighed eighty-four kilos. Does she herself ever wonder if that big man was really inside her at one time? Where was I conceived? Probably in the old double bed, that mahogany set with the attached bedside table, the bulkiest piece of furniture in the apartment, a massive schooner.

The girl is taking away the food tray. My mother had no appetite for the dessert, prune pudding with cream.

"This is Jónas Ebeneser, my son," I hear my mother say.

"Yes, I think you introduced us yesterday, Mom . . ."

The girl has no recollection of that, because she wasn't on duty yesterday.

"Jónas means 'dove' and Ebeneser 'the helpful one.' I got to choose the names," Mom continues.

It dawns on me that perhaps I should have asked the guy at Tryggvi's Tattoo Parlour to place a dove beside the lily; the two doves together, me and the bird, both with a few greying hairs.

I hope the girl will have vanished before the recounting of my birth begins. But she's not leaving because she puts down the tray now and starts to arrange the towels.

"Your birth was more difficult than your brother's" is the next thing my mother says. "Because of the size of your head. It was as if you had two horns on your forehead, two stumps," she explains, "like a bull calf."

The girl gawks at me. I know she is comparing mother and son.

I smile at her.

She smiles back.

"You smelled different, you and your brother," Mom continues from her armchair. "You smelled of clay, a cold and wet smell, cold cheeks, you were muddy around the mouth and came home with cat scratches on the back of your hands. They didn't heal well."

She stalls as if trying to remember her next cue in a script.

"My Pumpkin wrote an essay about potatoes when he was just eleven years old and called the essay 'Mother Earth.' It was about me, the essay . . ."

"Mom, I'm not sure she's interested in . . . Sorry, what's your name?"

"Diljá."

"I'm not sure Diljá is interested in this, Mom . . ."

On the contrary, the girl seems to be genuinely interested in what Mom has to say. Nodding sympathetically, she leans against the doorframe.

"It's incredible when you look at this hulk of a man today and think of how sensitive he was."

25

"Mom . . ."

"If there was a bird with a broken wing in the garden he'd weep . . . He was an open wound . . . Always worried about whether people were being good enough to each other . . . When I'm big, he said, I want to mend the world . . . because the world was suffering, because the world needed to be taken care of . . . My Pumpkin was always so fond of the twilight . . . when the shadows fell, he lay on the floor by the window and stared at the clouds and sky . . . so musical . . . Then he locked himself in to make a puppet theatre . . . made marionettes out of wet newspapers, painted them and sewed clothes onto them, locked the door and stuffed the keyhole with toilet paper . . . When he was a teenager he was still worried sick about the world . . . I'm not going to get married unless I fall in love, he said . . . Then he fell for Gudrún, a nurse and the head of a ward, who then became a midwife too, and took a course in management . . ."

"Mom . . ."

Smothered by the stuffiness of the hot room I walk towards the window that overlooks the lake, a set of red lights from last Christmas blink relentlessly on the windowsill. Draped over the window, which is forbidden to be opened to allow in even the slightest draft of cold air, are the living room curtains that Mom brought with her from our old house in Silfurtún and shortened. I recognise the pattern. From that vantage point one can observe a hearse backing out with its daily cargo.

"My little Gudrún Waterlily was conceived between two tussocks at the end of May, as freckled as a golden plover's egg, and highly educated on sea matters, and with some boyfriend who is a rapper and chews tobacco and wears an earring, not a normal earring, but some ginormous piercing with a whole spool of thread, a good-natured guy from the fishing village of Eskifjördur who watched over his granny when she was on her deathbed . . ."

"Mom, we get the picture . . ."

"Some men never recover after being jilted . . ."

"You can't trust everything she says," I say and open the window.

Then it's as if she were about to recount something, but can no longer remember what she was going to say and she fades like a transmitter that has lost its signal. For a moment she has vanished into another world and another time, where she is trying to navigate through a foggy landscape, to find a guiding star. She is a young girl who has lost her sheep and casts her misty gaze around the room, old faces slowly filing past the barren landscape.

The girl silently ducks out the door and my mother tries to adjust her hearing aid, to tune into my wavelength, into the earth's magnetic field, the correct time frequency.

I stand by the bookshelves and glance at the titles: *War and Peace* by Tolstoy, *A Farewell to Arms* by Hemingway, Erich Maria Remarque's *All Quiet on the Western Front*, Elie Wiesel's *Night*, *This Way for the Gas, Ladies and Gentlemen* by Tadeusz

Borowski, *Sophie's Choice* by William Styron, *Fatelessness* by Imre Kertész, *Saying Yes to Life in Spite of Everything* by Viktor Frankl, Primo Levi's *If This Is a Man*. I pull Paul Celan's collection of poems off the shelf and flip to "Death Fugue": "we drink you at night / we drink and drink." I slip the book into my pocket and pull out the *First World War*.

"Since you came out of your mother's womb there have been 568 wars," says the voice from the armchair.

It is difficult to know when my mother is actually with us because she's like an electrical current that comes and goes, or should I say a flickering candle. Just as I'm thinking she's extinguished, she unexpectedly flares up again.

Once the girl has left, I help my mother into bed. I hold her under the arm and she drags her slippers along the light green linoleum. What does she weigh? Forty kilos? It would take less than a gust to knock her over, the slightest breeze, even a puff of air would completely flatten her. I push two embroidered cushions aside and sit on the edge of her bed for a moment. She lies down and her body disappears into the mattress. The perfume I gave her is on the bedside table, "Eternity Now," because my mother likes to dab the back of her ears with the hereafter. She holds my hand, blue veins, the worldly-wise back of her hand, her nails are polished once a week.

Mom was the one who helped me with maths when I was in secondary school and she couldn't understand why it wasn't a piece of cake for everyone.

"Equations are a cinch," she'd say.

And she explained to me how I could work out square roots without using a pocket calculator. She said the square root of 2 ($\sqrt{2}$) is the number that gives two when it is multiplied by itself. We are therefore looking for an unknown number x, which is therefore $x \cdot 2 = 2$. We see that x is between 1.4 and 1.5 because $1.4^2 = 1.96 < 2$ but $1.5^2 = 2.25 > 2$. The next step is to look at the numbers between 1.40, 1.41, 1.42, and so on up to 1.49. It turns out that $1.41^2 = 1.9881 < 2$ and $1.42^2 = 2.0164 > 2$. This demonstrates that the square root of two is somewhere between 1.41 and 1.42.

"Have they negotiated a truce?" I hear her ask from the bed.

She gets her hair done once a week and the spring sun pouring through the western window illuminates her beautifully shaped light purple hair; she is a ball of fluff in the sunrays.

"Sixty million killed in World War II," she continues.

Talking to Mom is like talking to no one. That suits me fine, it's enough for me to feel the warmth from another living body. I decide that she understands me and come straight to the point.

"I'm unhappy," I say.

She pats the back of my hand.

"We all have our battles to fight," she says, before adding: "Napoleon was exiled from himself. Josephine was lonely in her marriage, just like me."

On top of the bookcase is a row of framed photographs, most of them of my daughter, Waterlily, at various ages. Two are of me and two of my brother, Logi, both equally represented. In one of the pictures I'm four years old and standing on a chair, hanging on to my mother's neck. She is wearing a light blue sweater and dark red lipstick and a white pearl necklace. I have a brush haircut, like a hedgehog, and have one bandaged arm in a sling. This is my oldest memory; they had to nail the arm together. Mom stands by the organ. What was being celebrated? Was it her birthday? I see now, as I peer at the picture, that there is a Christmas tree in the background. It's been forty-five years since that photograph was taken and the boy's expression is genuine and sincere.

The other picture is a confirmation photo. My lips are slightly parted and I'm staring at the photographer in bewilderment, as if a stranger had woken me up, as if I had yet to feel my way in the world that I'd been born into. It was a world made of teak with floral wallpaper in every room; apart from that it was all in black and white, like the TV.

I make one final attempt:

"I don't know who I am. I'm nothing and I own nothing."

"Your father didn't live through the Iranian war, nor the Iraqi war, nor Afghanistan, nor Ukraine, nor Syria . . . nor the Kárahnjúkar power plant protests, nor the roadwork that doubled the width of the Miklabraut highway . . ."

She stretches across the bedside table and pulls out some red lipstick.

Shortly after that I hear her launch into the Nordic king sagas:

" . . . Haakon Athelstan, Harald Bluetooth, Sweyn Forkbeard, Cnut the Great, Harald Fairhair, Eric Bloodaxe, Olaf Tryggvason . . ." she rattles off.

She is getting agitated and tells me she's busy.

"I'm a bit busy, Pumpkin dear."

The news is about to start and she half rises to turn on the radio and tackle the war of the day in the news summary, after which she will lie down with the death notices and funeral announcements in her ear.

When I leave, I call the help line to let them know there is a goose with a broken wing at the old folk's home.

"A male bird," I say. "Alone. With no mate."

And then I try to remember, didn't Hemingway shoot himself with his favourite rifle?

. . . the scepticism of manliness,
related to the genius for war
and conquest

The guy at the tattoo parlour had told me that my skin would be sore for a few days and that I could expect it to redden, or possibly even to itch and burst into a rash. If the skin started to swell and I developed a fever, I might need to take antibiotics or, in the worst-case scenario, go to an emergency room. I wouldn't be surprised if I were already experiencing the first symptoms.

Svanur is polishing the Opel when I get back from Mom's, the caravan sits ready in the driveway. He is wearing sandals and an orange fleece jacket, emblazoned with the logo of the tyre company he briefly worked for a few years ago. We met when he was working at Steel Legs Ltd., and it was actually Svanur who told me about the vacant attic apartment on this street, opposite his and Aurora's place. Apart from that, we're not close. At the moment he's convalescing at home, recovering from a slipped disc operation. Two "stay-at-home men" is what he calls us.

He has set up two folding chairs on the sidewalk, as if he were expecting a guest, and beckons me over.

I get the feeling that my neighbour has been watching me; when I came out this morning he was lingering near the dustbins with his dog and watching my front door.

Over the past few days his visits have also multiplied; he needed to borrow a wrench of a specific size and then returned it and asked me to help him lift the new fridge he just bought for the caravan. First and foremost, though, he wants to chat about what occupies his entire brain: motorised vehicles and the status of women in the world, two fields of interest that he tries to combine as much as possible. He drags over one of the folding chairs and signals me to sit. I have no alternative but to chat with my neighbour.

"People don't take good enough care of their cars" is the first thing he says to me. "We live on an island that's blasted by the sea and rusts the chassis. It's not enough to spray it once a year and change the oil; you've also got to polish it regularly. Three coats of polish and rubs in between. It's just garbage the stuff they use in those car washes."

He leans on the other folding chair.

"Some people drive on punctured tyres for years and end up having to change the whole wheel."

Svanur doesn't do conversations, but instead delivers monologues without looking at me, gazing somehow beyond me, as if the person he were really talking to were somehow beside or above me.

"When you think about how women are treated in the world, it makes you ashamed to be a man," he continues.

He straddles the chair and leans forward, pressing his elbows against his knees.

It transpires that Svanur has subscribed to some foreign TV channels and last night he watched a documentary about the circumcision of women and a current affairs programme about women and war.

"You've got a daughter . . ."

"Yes."

"Did you know that women do 90 percent of all the work on earth, but only own 1 percent of its assets? And what do men do in the meantime?"

He doesn't wait for an answer and continues:

33

"They dawdle, get drunk, and wage war."

He holds his big blacksmith's hands up to his face, his fingers greased with oil.

"Do you know how many women are raped every hour?"

"In the world, you mean?"

"In the world, yes."

"No."

"Seventeen thousand five hundred."

We both fall silent.

Then he continues.

"And do you know how many women will die giving birth tomorrow, Tuesday, May the sixth?"

"No."

"About two thousand."

He draws a deep breath.

"And as if it weren't enough for them to die giving birth, they have to endure forced marriages."

He removes his glasses, which are as thick as the bottom of a bottle and haven't been polished for ages. He says that he's short-sighted and astigmatic and that, if he takes off his glasses, the outline of the volcano on the other side of the bay goes fuzzy. He looks straight at me for the first time.

"We who are in the know and do nothing are the guilty ones."

There is a swarm of small birds in the garden, they fly off the roof, under the drainpipe, and vanish in an instant. I stand up and he then tells me there's an American chocolate cake in the oven and he's wondering if I'd like to pop in.

"Betty Crocker," he adds. And after a moment's hesitation: "Aurora is on a gluten-free diet."

So Svanur bakes.

He says that he just stuck the cake into the oven and that it should be ready in a short while.

I think it over. I have yet to borrow the hunting rifle from him.

"It's good for men to have someone to confide in," I hear him saying.

I tell him I'll be over soon.

I first need to pop into my apartment to check on something.

I am a watercolour.
I wash off

This morning half a mountain is visible through the kitchen window, as well as a stretch of the cold green sea; the mountain vanishes as yet another floor is added to the high-rise that is being built.

I turn on the computer and Google famous writers who have killed themselves. The number of pages on this subject surprises me. I would never have imagined there was such a large group of famous men and women who decided at some point to put an end to their lives. My recollection was correct: the author of *The Sun Also Rises* and *To Have and Have Not* had used his favourite rifle. Nor do I need much time to confirm my suspicion that most men shoot themselves, although it is more prevalent in countries where gun ownership is more widespread. I scroll down a page and see that a short story writer shot himself with a shotgun in the middle of a ski slope and painted it red, and a thirty-year-old poet first shot his young mistress and then himself; when he was discovered in his hotel room in Paris, his toenails were painted red and a cross was tattooed on one of his soles. Few leap out of windows, although several leap off bridges into rivers, and some rivers are more popular than others, such as the Seine, for example. I see that one of the people who drowned in the Seine was Paul Celan, the author of the collection of poetry on my mother's shelf, which I still have in my jacket pocket. The Roman poet Petronius slit his wrists and then bandaged them again in order to delay his death so that he could listen to his friend reciting poems about life. Sleeping pills also feature as a way of enabling people to sleep longer than usual in hotel rooms, for eternity you might say.

I note with interest that women apply other methods, focusing more on gas ovens in the kitchen or exhaust fumes in sealed garages after a few shots of vodka.

I also notice that it's the women who are more prone to leaving farewell notes, they write a few lines: *For my lover, returning to his wife* and say of themselves: *As for me, I am a watercolour. I wash off.* Virginia Woolf left a love letter to her husband before she filled her pockets with stones and walked into the River Ouse. *I don't think two people could have been happier,* she wrote. Other farewells were simple, such as the poet who jumped off a boat in the Gulf of Mexico exclaiming: *Goodbye, everybody!*

What strikes me is the fact that these men and women were generally younger than me, by as much as two decades. The years before or after thirty are the most difficult. One decides to end it at the age of thirty-two and another at thirty-three, both novelists; there is also a thirty-four-year-old painter; Mayakovsky reaches the age of thirty-six; Pavese was forty-one. Turning thirty-seven is difficult for an artist and not everyone overcomes that hurdle. Musicians are even younger: Brian Jones, Jimi Hendrix, Janis Joplin, Kurt Cobain, Amy Winehouse, and Jim Morrison were all twenty-seven years old. I've passed the dying age of artists.

Other laws apply when you're just ordinary.

About to turn forty-nine

Male

Divorced

Heterosexual

Powerless

With no sex life

A handyman

A scar is an abnormal skin formation that
has grown around a wound or lesion

Svanur stands on the chequered kitchen floor in his socks and his "Shit Happens" T-shirt and ties his apron.

I watch him slip on red oven mitts, open the oven, cautiously pull out the rack with the baking mould, and stick a needle thermometer into the cake.

"Another seven minutes," he says, before pouring cream into a bowl and plugging in the mixer. He turns his back to me as he concentrates on the task. Once he has whipped the cream, he rinses the whisks and sticks them into the dishwasher.

I consider the right moment to raise the issue of the rifle.

While he is scooping the cream out of the bowl with a spatula, he says he has noticed a certain restlessness in Aurora's soul.

He still has his back turned to me.

"You never know what a woman is thinking. They betray nothing on the surface, then suddenly they make a decision and tell you they don't love you anymore. Like they've secretly been changing."

He takes the cake out of the oven, frees it from the mould, cuts a slice, and then meticulously examines the wound to ensure it is fully baked. Once that's done, he cautiously places the slice on my plate with the pastry server, propped up by his stubby fingers.

He seems anxious and wants to know if there were any signs in the air before Gudrún left me.

I give this some thought.

"She told me I repeated everything she said."

He is flabbergasted.

"Repeated, how do you mean?"

"Yeah, she told me that when she said something to me, I would answer by repeating what she'd just said. For example, by changing an affirmation into a question."

Svanur's face is one big question mark.

I explain.

"When she said, 'Waterlily phoned,' then I would answer, 'Yeah, Waterlily phoned?' That's called repetition, she said."

Svanur looks at me as if I'd proposed a new theory on the laws of black hole physics and time.

"Isn't it okay to repeat?" he asks hesitantly.

"No, Gudrún didn't think so."

"And what should one say—instead of repeating?"

"I'm not sure."

"Did you ask her not to leave?"

"No, I didn't."

He grabs a milk carton from the fridge, pours two glasses, and pushes one over to me. My mother sometimes saves a glass of milk for me with a slice of brown-butter layer cake with white buttercream on a plate on her beside table; the milk is lukewarm out of the steel flask that is actually meant for coffee, I know the taste.

39

We are both silent.

Then my neighbour picks up the thread.

"Now you're a womaniser."

I ask myself whether I've misheard him or whether he might attribute some other meaning to that word than I do. But Svanur isn't the type to speak in metaphors.

Should I tell him that I haven't touched a woman's bare flesh—not deliberately at least—not held a woman with both hands for eight years and five months, or since Gudrún and I stopped having sex together, and that apart from my mother, ex-wife, and daughter—the three Gudrúns—there are no women in my life. There is no shortage of bodies in this world, however, and they occasionally have the power to stir me and remind me that I am a man. A woman steps out of a hot tub, water trickles down her flesh and the mounting steam engulfs her; it's close to freezing outside and the half-moon wading through the clouds enters the scene just before the swimming pool closes. It's also possible that I may have unwittingly grazed bare arms in a short-sleeved shirt while I was queuing in a store, or that a woman's hair may have touched me as she was bending over; the girl who cuts my hair springs to mind, for example. When she shampoos me at the sink, she stands behind me, massages me around the temples and says I have good hair. I once asked her what she was thinking and she laughed, looking at me through the mirror, and answered: a certain man and recipe. No, I would need to shoot myself, to shred my flesh with a steel bullet to feel the body. That's what men do.

"Because some of Aurora's friends were asking whether you were chasing skirt. She asked me and I told her that you're not chasing skirt at the moment. They asked Aurora if you were over your wife yet and she asked me and I told her you weren't. They wanted to know whether you frequented cafés or the theatre and I said I didn't think so. They asked if you're a reader and I told Aurora that you are, so she told them and they seemed to be quite excited by that and wanted to know what kind of books and I said novels and poetry, and they wanted to know Icelandic or foreign and I said both."

Before I know it, I've popped the question:

"I was wondering if you could lend me a rifle. For the weekend."

If my request has caught him off guard, he isn't showing any sign of it. Instead he nods, takes off the apron, and places it on the back of the chair, as if he had been waiting for me to mention the weapon. He vanishes into the living room and I hear him rummaging through a locked cupboard. In the meantime, I examine two photographs on the fridge, one of Svanur in a fleece jacket with the dog by his side and the other of Aurora in a group of smiling women. They're in outdoor gear and hiking boots and half of the group is kneeling as if it were a photo of a football team. After a short while he returns with the rifle

41

and leans it against the wall, beside the mop. He motions towards the pictures.

"Once the caravan is fixed, Aurora and I can find our own patch of moss by any babbling brook we want."

He then sits opposite me at the table and pours himself another glass of milk.

I hear him say that he suspects Aurora has started to read poetry.

"When I slipped past her through the bathroom door last night, she said that I was *eclipsing her horizon*."

He shakes his head.

"Sometimes I feel it's better to think about Aurora than have her beside me. She'd never understand that."

He has his elbows on the table, hands in front of his face, and speaks between his fingers.

"Aurora doesn't realise that a man has got stuff going on inside. That a man has a feeling for beauty. Oil leaks from the car onto the wet asphalt and the rainbow colours make me dream of another reality."

I stand up, take the shotgun, and Svanur escorts me to the front steps. I hold the weapon under my arm, with the barrel pointing down.

Should I tell him how things are, that I'm not going to grow old?

Does he suspect that?

If I were to ask Svanur to give me just one reason why I should continue to live.

I'd only ask for one, but it could be two.

By way of explanation, I'd say that I'm lost.

Would he then say: I know what you mean, I don't know who I am either. And embrace me in the gap of the hall door, half inside and half out, his body framed in a rectangular halo, over a hundred kilos, in a T-shirt tucked into his trousers at the front and hanging out at the back. Two middle-aged men locked in an embrace on the steps in front of the entrance, the fifth of the fifth?

Aurora would call out: "Who's there? If they're selling dried fish or prawns, take the prawns. Don't buy any liquorice. It's not good for you."

What could Svanur say that would be a revelation to me?

Would he look for some appropriate poetic or philosophical quotation on death? Would he find the words to change the situation? Or would he just say:

"You'll die soon enough anyway. You can be sure of that. Talk to me again in thirty years' time and then you'll be clinging to every minute like a dog to a bone. Like your mom."

Instead he says:

"Have I shown you the scar already?"

"The scar? No, what scar?"

"From the slipped disc operation."

Before I know it, he's yanking his T-shirt out of his trousers and pulling it up behind. There are few people on the street in the middle of a workday.

A large scar stretches along his spine. I picture how the guy at Tryggvi's Tattoo Parlour would tackle this with a quad bike or snowmobile, but I resist the temptation to reveal my water lily.

"Did you know," he says, "that in some places in the world scars are symbols that command respect and a person who bears a big and impressive scar is a person who has looked a wild beast in the eye, tackled his fears, and survived?"

I walk across the street with the rifle under my arm, up to the fourth floor, and lay it on the double bed.

Most scars on the skin are flat and pale in colour
and only retain a small portion of the wound
that caused their formation

I just got through the door when the phone in my pocket rings.

It's the nursing home. A messenger. The woman apologetically introduces herself as a member of the staff who is helping my mother make a phone call. My mother was expecting me today but I didn't show up. She says this hesitantly and cautiously, as if she knows it's only been two hours since I visited Mom and that I seldom visit less than three times a week. She passes the phone to Mom. My lunchtime visit has been erased from her mind.

Mom's voice quivers on the line:

"This is Gudrún Stella Jónasdóttir Snæland, can I speak to Jónas?"

"It's me, Mom."

"Is that you, Jónas?"

"Yes, this is my number you called, Mom dear." She wants to know why I never visit her.

I tell her I came today.

She mulls this over and, while she tries to get her bearings, I hang on the line.

When she comes back to me she says she remembers my visit well, but forgot to ask me something when I was there. If I have a saw. The job she wants to ask me to do is to remove the branch of a tree that keeps knocking against a window by her bed and prevents her from sleeping.

"Your father kept his toolbox in our bedroom. He was a reliable man, your father, even though he wasn't much fun."

She hesitates.

"Did you say you were going on a journey?"

"No."

"Didn't you say you were going to war?"

"No, not that either."

She dithers again.

"Are you going on a special mission, Pumpkin dear?"

Special mission. I think about that term. Like to save the planet. Discover a new vaccine?

"No."

45

There is yet another long silence on the phone. Maybe she's trying to remember why she called.

"Don't you want to live, Pumpkin dear?"

"I'm not sure."

"At least you still have all your hair. The men on my side don't lose their hair."

Before I know it, I've said it:

"Gudrún Waterlily isn't mine."

I could have added she isn't the blood of my blood. I haven't procreated anything, the line dies out with me.

I hear rustling at the other end and voices in the distance that seem to be drawing closer. There is a prolonged silence before she continues:

"Your father and I visited a history museum on our honeymoon. That was about as romantic as it got. But what struck me the most was that the soldiers' uniforms were made out of such thin material. Made out of lousy sheets, all for show."

"I know, Mom."

I sense there is something still bothering her.

"Who's Heidegger?" Mom finally asks.

Didn't I once write an essay about Heidegger in my only year at university? Wasn't he the one who claimed that humanity's relationship with reality should grow out of a sense of wonderment? Like a child or a young animal.

"A German philosopher. Why do you ask?"

"Because he phoned this morning and was asking for you. I told him he had the wrong number."

Apologia pro vita sua
(*A defence of one's own life*)

A number of other options were certainly considered. It occurs to me, for example, that I could take down the ceiling light and use the hook. A decision also has to be made about the location. I stage different scenarios in my mind. Should I shoot myself in the living room or hang myself in the bedroom, kitchenette, or bathroom? I also have to choose what clothes to wear. What would be appropriate? Pyjamas, Sunday best, work clothes, in my socks or shoes?

Suddenly I remember that Waterlily has a key and might barge in on me. It would be typical of her to be standing there in the middle of the living room out of the blue to share something she had just discovered. She would say:

"Dad, did you know that bird couples only migrate to this island once and therefore can't draw any lessons from the experience?"

How long would it take for her to start worrying about me? What's more, she'd be the one who would have to go through my stuff. I think of the basement downstairs, which is full of junk that should have been sorted and thrown away long ago. Shouldn't I spare her the burden?

As soon as I open the basement door, I see the stool I designed and built when Gudrún and I started living together. It has an adjustable seat that can be raised and lowered. There's the toboggan and the orange tent that takes the better part of a day to put up, sleeping bags and hiking shoes. I haven't been down in this basement since I moved into the block and I sidestep my way between the boxes. One of them is marked with Mom's wobbly handwriting: "Tea set, to go to Jónas." On a shelf there is a dollhouse I built for Waterlily and, next to it, the old record player. I'd forgotten that.

A large toolbox lies in the centre of the floor, containing various tools I rarely use: a selection of chisels, a ball-peen hammer, a number of Phillips screwdrivers, handsaws, putty spatulas, a fretsaw, a carpenter's plane, an angle, a compass, rasps, files, three carpenter's rulers. I have a claw hammer and screwdrivers of various types and sizes in the toolbox I keep under the sink or in the trunk of the car. It also contains a drill, the first tool I bought after I met Gudrún. We rented a basement flat in the Furumelur district that had a ruined linoleum floor, so I read up on it and managed to lay down a parquet on my own. Once I'd learned that, I found out how to tile, wallpaper, and change the plumbing. I thought in metres, length and width, 170 times 80 or 92 times 62. I agree with my mother when she says it's easier to express suffering in numbers than in longing, but when

I think of beauty I nevertheless think of 4,252 grams and 52 centimetres.

Far in the corner lies a battered cardboard box, carefully taped and labelled THROW AWAY with a black felt-tip marker. If I remember correctly, this is the box that was also supposed to be thrown away in the last and second-to-last move and it has remained unopened in several cellars. Why is it still here then? I fetch a box cutter from my toolbox, splice through the tape, and lift the lids. It seems to be mostly university books from my only year at university. I pick up *Beyond Good and Evil* by Nietzsche and skim through a pile of typed essays and handwritten glossaries. In the middle of the box there is a brown envelope. I open it and pull out a twenty-seven-year-old newspaper cutting with a yellowed obituary about my father. It's written by one of his friends, who offers condolences to his surviving wife. He also mentions his two sons, Logi, the living image of his father, doing his final year in Business Studies, and Jónas, who has his mother's talent for music and is taking his first year in Philosophy. It occurs to me that in just two weeks I'll be the same age as Dad was when he collapsed on the doorstep. Maybe the same genetic defect will spare me the bother?

"I looked out the kitchen window and saw your father staggering and I thought he was drunk," said Mom. "When I came out he was lying on the path. They took him away and left me on my own.

"Some people don't follow you all the way," she added.

That same evening, Mom removed Dad's shirts from the hangers on his side of the wardrobe and piled them up on their bed.

"Don't you want to wait with that, Mom?" I asked. "At least until the funeral?"

We gave all the clothes away and because Mom didn't want to run into anyone wearing his coat, I was sent off with four bags of his clothes to a neighbouring town.

It used to get on my nerves when Dad would ask how I was getting on at school, I even suspected he was secretly researching the subject. That hunch was confirmed when we were going through his stuff; he had ordered a book entitled *How to Ask Clever Questions about Nietzsche*.

I slip the obituary back into the envelope and dig deeper in the box. At the bottom there are three worn-out notebooks. I open one of them and recognise the immature handwriting. Scrawled. Are these the diaries I wrote when I was around twenty? I skim through them and according to the dates, they span three years—with intervals.

THROW AWAY. That box is going into the garbage. I pick up another and rapidly browse through it, pausing here and there. As far as I can make out, it's divided between descriptions of clouds, weather, and trips with women. The philosophy student's quotations from Plato's *Symposium* immediately set the tone on the first page and show that I managed to focus on the essentials in my studies:

"All men possess a procreative instinct, both physically and mentally, and when our bodies reach a certain age they feel an urge to reproduce."

Each entry starts with a date followed by a description of the weather, like an old farmer's almanac: *2 March. Still, sunny, temperature -3 degrees. 26 April. Strong winds, temperature 4 degrees. 12 May. Gentle southeastern breeze, temperature 7 degrees.* Closely connected to these weather reports are entries in which I describe various types of cloud formations and contemplate heavenly bodies. *Wind-sculpted altocumulus.* When did I stop thinking about clouds? Followed by: *It is considered possible that a new moon may be circling the earth. However, several experts believe it is more likely to be the fragment of a rocket in motion.*

And among the long-extinguished stars in the middle of the cosmos, a shopping list rotates on an elliptical path by the celestial pole:

Buy strawberry yogurt and condoms.

But I don't have to go far to realise that descriptions of female bodies and relationships with women make up the lion's share of the entries. It seems I refer to girlfriends by their initials and thank them for sleeping with me. *Thanks, K* appears on one page, *Thanks, D* on another. Sometimes the initial is underlined. *Thanks, M.* M appears twice and so does K, with some months in between. Was it the same K? The accounts contain parenthetical asides. *L (pure virgin).* I had spent several summers in the country at my maternal uncle's sheep farm and drew my analogies from the valley

51

of the glacier: *(K's skin is as smooth as a lamb's lungs)*. Two days later it's S. I desperately try to remember. For the first time in my life I had a chance with girls and I remember a woman looking at me and me thinking: this could work. I flick between entries. G seems to be the last letter in the flesh alphabet, is that Gudrún? I'm twenty-two years old when I thank G for sleeping with me and, as far as I can tell, it happened on a mountain climb. *(G has a recent scar from an appendix operation but I didn't mention it)* I wrote in brackets.

I skim through the notebook in search of a particular date:

11 October 1986.

Cycled home from school. On my way to Silfurtún, I see Reagan and Gorbachev on the steps of Höfdi House. They're both wearing coats, one a trench coat and the other with a furry collar. There were also three geese in the field. I saw them on TV that night, in black and white, like sand and a glacier. Then I wrote and underlined the words: *I was there.*

A day later I wrote on the same page:

12 October. Dad is dead.

The world is not the same.

I extend my life by three days and borrow Svanur's trailer to empty the basement.

I take three trips up to the apartment, one with the stool, another with the record player, and the final one with the cardboard box marked THROW AWAY.

The higher we soar,
the smaller we appear to those who cannot fly

I peep into the fridge to see what's there: two eggs in a carton marked "from our most experienced hens." In the cupboard there is a packet of fusilli pasta, how long should they be boiled, don't they tend to swell up? On the windowsill there's a parsley plant that I've been trying to keep alive, mostly withered now. I scramble the eggs and clip the green stems over the pan.

While the pasta is boiling, I peruse the last pages in the squared diary.

One entry stands out, due to its length, three whole pages of uninterrupted text. I seem to be describing a mountain climb and I have added an underlined title, as if it were a short story: _Climbing the steps of the initiation temple_. According to the date it's June the seventh and I'm not travelling alone because the entry opens with: _G asked to come along._

Borrowed the Subaru from Mom after choir practice (broken exhaust pipe). Have had my eye on this mountain for some time (longer than on G). Have slept with four girls in the choir and morale is low. The choirmaster (a friend of Mom's) pulled me aside and told me the tension was affecting the voices.

I seem to make amends by inviting the fifth girl on a drive and mountain hike.

G was wearing a yellow polo-neck and white plimsolls.

53

And, as usual, I detail the shopping list: *On the way we stopped at a shop and I bought prawn salad sandwiches, two Cokes, and two Prince Polo chocolate bars.*

In the car on the way to the crater I tell G that Dad died this winter and that I dropped out of school to take over the family company, Steel Legs Ltd. I tell her that I live with Mom and have one older brother. I also tell her I intend to become a father one day. (Why did I say that? I felt I had to say that.) I tell her about some of the things that have happened in the past and also more recently, which explain my way of thinking and feeling today. This is followed by a sentence that I've underlined twice: *I spoke and G was silent.*

Then there are five lines of text that I scribbled over and that are totally illegible until the mountain reappears:

G started to betray doubts when she saw the mountain rise above us and all the rocks. I walked ahead and she followed in my footsteps and I could feel her breath on my neck. It was foggy and difficult to find the top rock. We waited for the mist to clear so that I could offer G a glimpse of the glacier to the east. We did it on the way back. It had rained and the moss was wet and we didn't take off any more clothes than necessary. It was slightly more complicated for her because she was wearing some kind of dungarees. I heard the flutter of a ptarmigan nearby and thought: What does a bird see, what does a bird think? A sheep was suddenly standing beside us and staring and I told G to close her eyes.

And I thought, what does a sheep see, what does a sheep think? As we were putting our clothes back on, G said, "Imagine if an eruption were to start underneath us."

On the way back to the car, we took a shortcut across an arctic tern nesting area.

Thousands of arctic terns.

A choir of a thousand voices.

There I threw up my prawn salad sandwich.

Because I was feeling weak, G offered to drive back into town and I lay on the backseat. G talked and I was silent. She told me about her mother and her nursing course and how difficult it was to find a good vein to stick a needle into. On the way she stopped the car on one occasion and explained that there were some young ptarmigans on the road.

Then the account peters out. I'm at the bottom of the mountain again. Or that's what it says in clear letters: *I've reached the foot of the mountain.* I turn the page and the next entry is a month later, when I visit G.

7 July.

Met G again at her and her mother's home. Saw her completely naked for the first time (not just in portions). It was impossible to lock the bedroom door so I had to drag a chest of drawers in front of it. Before I left she told me she was expecting a baby.

I asked her how that could have happened and she answered that condoms aren't foolproof.

I was still growing up and I was expecting a child. I lived with Mom and slept in a single bed with a linen drawer I got as a confirmation gift. The report on what my flesh produced on my behalf ends with two sentences on the next page: *A baby was conceived on the mountain witnessed by a sheep. A few feet away from a dormant crater.*

55

A baby was conceived on the mountain
witnessed by a sheep

All of a sudden Gudrún had knit me a sweater and I thought, we've become a couple. She handed it to me, ironed and folded, and said, "It matches your eyes." Then she started knitting a rib stitch for the baby. We sat on the sofa at her place in the evenings, watched TV and ate popcorn with her mother. I'd spent four summers on my uncle's sheep farm and knew what was in store for her, I had lambing experience, had dragged out their slimy bodies. I remember I tried to bring a horned ram into the world, to get the horns past the canal, I can still hear the mother's bleating.

A little over eight months after the mountain hike, Gudrún Waterlily was born on an intercalary day, two weeks before her time and with soft nails. As was to be expected, the baby lay crosswise in the womb and could not be turned, so a caesarean was performed. I was terrified when the midwife approached me with the child, she taught me how to create a shell around the tiny body, I held a life in my hands, the most fragile creature in the world, and I thought, she'll outlive me.

I skip to the last pages in the book until I find the following sentence:

29 February. She will outlive me. Eyelids like transparent butterfly wings.

Then I had to pop into work after lunch to handle an order. Why did I do that? Because a man called to tell me he'd be collecting his order at one-thirty.

I was the first of my friends to tie the knot, which meant regular sex at home, I had access to a female body every night. I quickly got used to it. Initially, after the birth, Gudrún wanted to choose the parts of her body I had access to. I wasn't allowed to hold her stomach, I wasn't allowed to go near her C-section scar. "Put your hand here," she said. "No, not like that, keep it still, don't move or breathe so heavily." I tried to hold onto her shoulders or to let my hands rest on her rib cage right under her breasts, but sometimes I forgot the things I wasn't allowed to do, groping my way, searching for a path to follow along her naked flesh, and my hands slid down to her tummy.

"What?" she would then say.

"Nothing," I answered.

"No, because you're holding my tummy."

Twenty-six years later my wife tells me: "Waterlily isn't yours. I felt it was right that you should know, since we're breaking up." And then she adds: "I'd never met a guy who spoke about suffering and death on a first date. When you said we all die I felt that was something to build a life on. That was when I decided that Waterlily would be yours."

The last words I write in the diary are undated.

I am flesh.

After that I stopped keeping a record of my life.

By flesh I mean everything below my head. This is consistent with the fact that flesh is the beginning and end of all the most important things in my life: I was born and the heart and lungs started their relentless work, a child was born and I shouldered the responsibility of the flesh of my flesh, and soon my body will cease to work. It's as if I could hear Mom lecturing me on the order of the world: "You know, Jónas, the big story started long before we were born."

> Wounds heal at different speeds and the scars
> that are formed can lie at varying depths,
> some are deeper than others

It's a quarter past two in the morning and someone is knocking on my door on the fourth floor, first lightly, then more insistently.

Svanur stands on the landing, out of breath, and glances over my shoulder. The front door downstairs should be locked, but he said that he slipped in behind a neighbour who was coming home from a binge. He has been unable to sleep and, looking at my place, thought he could see some movement behind the blinds in my attic, someone walking about, and came to the conclusion that I was awake as well. He wants to invite me for a walk with his dog, who is waiting by the caravan downstairs.

Big girl, he calls his bitch.

Can I tell him I have other plans at this time of night?

Suddenly he has stepped into my place and entered the living room. He looks around, scanning the space swiftly and methodically. Is he checking me out?

His gaze freezes on the stool in the middle of the living room floor and the chandelier I've placed on the coffee table, but it's not as if I'm standing there with a belt in my hands.

I close the computer displaying the page of suicide methods of writers.

The contents of the box lie in a heap on the dining table.

"Are you tidying up?" he asks.

"Yes, I'm going through some old papers."

Before I know it, he has vanished into the bathroom. I hear him opening and closing cabinets and, on the way back, he peeps into the bedroom. The rifle is still lying on the double bed. He then opens the coat cupboard in the corridor, bringing his inspection to an end.

"I want to understand Aurora better," says my neighbour with a sigh.

MAN AND BEAST

Svanur holds onto the dog by its leash as we walk along a path that leads down to the harbour. The air is so still and there isn't a soul around at night, apart from a young father with a pram. Did I take Gudrún Waterlily out for walks at night when she had tummy aches to allow her mom to sleep?

Svanur breaks the silence.

"I find these bright nights so difficult," I hear him say. He bends down to clean up after the dog.

"You can recognise the types that don't carry a bag and think they can get away with it."

We stand on the pier, halfway between the whale-watching boats and the whale-hunting boats, the vast sky above us.

"Isn't that beautiful?" I hear Svanur ask.

I don't say anything. A magnificent spring sky with three horizontal orange streaks isn't powerful enough to provoke any longing in me; I saw the very same sky last year and the year before. I can prolong my existence or I can bring it to an end.

"We're so small," he says, patting the dog. Then he corrects himself:

"Man is so small."

We walk towards the lighthouse and Svanur says he walked the same way yesterday and spotted a seal. And the seal also spotted him. They had looked each other in the eye, man and animal. He wondered whether he should take a picture of the seal with his phone, but decided against it because he said to himself, man and animal, nothing more to say, no deeper meaning. Then, when he got home, he read an article online about a seal that had learned how to use a screwdriver.

"Is it a coincidence that I stumbled precisely on that article?" he asks, gazing beyond me, out at the vast green expanse.

We both fall silent.

The dog barks and wants to wade into the seaweed, but Svanur tugs on the leash. An arctic tern swirls above us and I wave it away with my hand. The nesting season has begun.

"Did you know," he says, still gazing out at the sea, "that humans are the only animals that shed tears to express feelings such as joy or sorrow?"

I say yes, isn't that due to the stimulation of the lachrymal gland?

"Unlike animals, we know that our lives end," my neighbour continues. "We cease to exist."

He looks around for a trash bin, but there are none in sight so he holds the bag all the way back.

As I'm about to say goodbye to Svanur, I sense there is still something weighing on his mind.

He shuffles his feet in front of the caravan.

"Did you need ammunition as well?" he asks.

"Yes."

"I suspected as much."

He hesitates.

"Unfortunately it got used up on the ptarmigan hunting last year."

He looks beyond me, the dog stares right at me.

"To be honest, I've never handled a shotgun before," I tell my neighbour.

"I thought as much. That you don't know how to fire a gun."

He's right, I can't fire a gun. Someone else might end up getting shot.

Then he asks if he can come over every now and then.

"Is it okay if I come over every now and then?"

I tell him I'm a bit busy the next few days, but before I know it, I've added:

"I'm about to leave. On a trip."

The idea strikes me like a bolt of lightning; I'll make myself vanish. That way I don't have to worry about Waterlily discovering my body. Like a bird spinning down a vortex, hovering horizontally for a few metres before it dives and perishes. One final wing flap before aiming for the gaping crevice, the whitened bones will serve as a landmark to travellers.

As I reflect on this further, however, I exclude the option of not being found; Waterlily would certainly spend her whole life searching for me, and ultimately the pain would be too much of a burden. Instead I would go on a trip abroad and Waterlily and Mom would get me back in a tidy box.

"Your father has gone on his longest journey," Mom had said to me. I had just come home from an exam and she was standing in the doorway, waiting for me.

"Gone where?" I asked, noticing that his brown briefcase was lying in the bed of pansies.

I took the briefcase into my bedroom, opened it, and arranged the bills on the desk. The next day I told Mom I had quit university and started working at Steel Legs Ltd., Father & Son. Society's interest in steel legs has been fairly constant over the decades.

"Don't worry," I said to Mom.

"The best moments in my life," I hear Svanur say, "are when I'm lying alone inside a sleeping bag up on a heath, holding my rifle at the crack of dawn, waiting for the birds to wake up. Remaining silent and staring at the crust of snow. It's like being inside a womb. One feels secure. One doesn't need to be born. One doesn't need to come out."

What did I say to Svanur?

I repeated what he said. I said no, one doesn't need to come out. That was the last sentence I spoke to him. Which means that my last word was "out."

The Word became flesh
and made his dwelling among us

I phone Waterlily and we arrange to meet. She suggests a bakery with two tables and chairs.

In our last conversation, she'd asked if I sorted my garbage and whether I'd got myself a blue recycling bin for paper. In return I asked how Sigtryggur was doing and she answered: "You mean Tristan, Dad?" and added:

"That's over."

My daughter doesn't need a father, but a boyfriend. My function has become obsolete.

She is wearing the blue hooded parka with fur trim I got her for Christmas and she gives me a broad smile. I remember when she got braces and cried a whole weekend. She takes off her parka and hangs it on the back of the chair.

My daughter is an expert on marine biology and wrote her final thesis on the damaging effects of plastic on the flora and fauna of the sea, and particularly on the sperm production of men.

"Perfluoro particles," she says, and I nod.

It's from her that I get all my knowledge of the impact climate change has on ocean acidification and hypoxia.

Then I remember that when she was small she had a burning interest in flowing water and turned on all the taps. She stood with her chin hanging over the rim of the sink or pulled up a chair, climbed on top of it, and watched the flow.

"Water runs," she said when she was two years old.

She wears her granny's watch with lots of bracelets over it. They meet every week, the two Gudrúns, granny and the granddaughter, and chat about their worries about warfare and the future of the world.

My daughter has some cocoa and a Danish pastry, and I have a coffee and a cake called "wedding bliss."

"Did you know," she says, "that last year the world spent 240 thousand billion krónur on weapons and arms?"

She sips from her cup and wipes the cream off her upper lip.

"We need to calculate the damage caused by the people who profit from war and make them pay for it," I hear her continue. "That way they would understand that war is much more expensive than peace. In any case, the only language they understand is money," she adds.

My daughter expresses herself with her entire body when she speaks, then she suddenly falls silent.

"Have you seen your granny?" I ask.

"Yes, and she agrees with me."

"I've no doubt she does."

We both laugh.

What kind of a father was I?

I was never bad to my daughter, never annoyed. I answered her questions and took her to football practice and watched her inside goals, with her skinny legs in green socks and her big goalie gloves, diving fearlessly on the ball.

Answer: I was an average father. Grade: 7.5.

I think about whether I should tell her that I'm going to embark on my longest journey.

"What, Dad?" she says. "You're looking at me in such a weird way."

65

"Nothing."

"Are you sure?"

"Yes, absolutely."

I wonder: Does she know? Has her Mom told her?

She looks at me searchingly.

"Are you sure everything is okay, Dad?"

"Yes, everything is fine."

"Have you heard from Mom?"

"No, nothing."

"But you're on good terms?"

"Yes, everything is fine."

She carefully scrutinises me.

"And you're not sad?"

"No, not sad."

I then wonder if she will forgive me. Or blame me, hate me even. Will she baptise her son in my name, will he be freckled like his mom, will he be a loner or an explorer?

"Dad, are you ill?"

"No, no, nothing like that."

She finishes the Danish pastry, collects the crumbs and deposits them on the plate.

"And you're not lonely?"

"No, no."

There is something she has to get off her chest.

"It's just that I had a dream the other night."

She hesitates.

"I dreamt I was giving birth to a big baby boy."

"I see."

"And he had an extra big head."

Should I tell her I haven't a clue of how to interpret dreams? She takes a deep breath.

"The problem was that the baby boy was you."

"How do you mean?"

"The baby in the dream. I was giving birth to my own father."

I do my best.

"Could this mean some new plan?"

"Yes, I looked it up and a birth can symbolise a rebirth or a new beginning, but also the part of one's self that is neglected. And the size of the head means that a neglected part of the self requires care and attention."

I hesitate.

"Have you found out what that means?"

I hear from her breathless voice that she is worried.

"In some cases a birth can signify a death."

"I see."

"But it doesn't necessarily have to be a physical death, but rather much more the end of one thing and the beginning of another." She finishes the cup of cocoa and we both slip into a silence. Then she turns to me:

"What about you, Dad, don't you dream?"

"No, I don't actually."

"Doesn't the son of an organ player ever dream of organ music?"

67

I smile at her.

"No, not even organ music."

Once she has finished putting on her parka, she remembers something.

"No, the problem is," she says as she adjusts the elastic in her hair, "that a cupboard door came off its hinges in the kitchen and fell, breaking a tile on the floor. Any chance of you taking a look at it for me?"

Waterlily rents a small apartment with a female friend of hers, and when they moved in, I sandpapered their kitchen unit, varnished them, and changed the handles. I also installed a shower instead of the old bathtub and placed tiles around it.

"Sure, no problem," I say.

I do what the three Gudrúns in my life ask me to do. I put up mirrors and shelves and carry furniture from place to place and put it down wherever they tell me. I have tiled seven bathrooms and installed five kitchen units, I can lay a parquet floor, and I've smashed double-glazed windows with a sledgehammer. I'm not a man who destroys things, however, but rather one who fixes things that are broken. If someone asks me why I do what I do, I answer that a woman asked me to.

I wrap my arms around my daughter and embrace her.

I intend to say something else to her but instead say:

"Did you know that humans are the only animals who cry?"

She smiles from ear to ear.

"No, I didn't know that. I thought we were the only animals who laugh."

When I get home I scan through the bookshelves looking for the book on the interpretation of dreams. Gudrún hasn't taken it with her because I find it on the same shelf as the manual on repairing teak furniture.

I look up *organ*.

To dream that one hears beautiful organ music is a sign of sexual energy and virility, the book claims.

"Dad, don't believe everything you think," Waterlily had said as we parted.

A ticket to the moon,
one way

The neighbourhood sinks into silence. But for the sound of a bird.

The question is where do I want to go.

I surf the Web in search of a suitable destination and focus on countries along warfare latitudes. Sixty-three countries and regions soon emerge as potential candidates. What was the country that Svanur mentioned in connection with the documentary he had watched about women and war?

In the end, I choose a country that was in the news for a long time because of the battles being waged there, but has vanished from the spotlight due to a cease-fire a few months ago. The situation is said to be precarious, and it is unclear whether the cease-fire will hold. It seems ideal, I could be shot on a street corner or step on a land mine. It's as if I could hear Svanur's voice:

"If you were a woman, you'd be raped first."

It will be a one-way ticket. I find a hotel online in some derelict small town I recognise from the news. I remember that hotels are, in fact, favoured venues for topping one's self. The online photos were clearly taken before the war, and one can see that the hotel once stood by a little square adorned with flowers, and that bee breeding and honey production thrived in the surrounding countryside. The hotel is situated close to the beach, and according to the information on the website, it was a popular tourist resort, known for its archaeological sites and mud baths. There is mention of thermal baths in the hotel and a centuries-old mosaic wall.

As I'm writing a farewell letter, I slip a record onto the turntable and listen to "One Way Ticket to the Moon."

Who should I address it to? To my daughter and mother, the two namesakes, Gudrún W. and Gudrún S.?

I start to think about what Svanur said on the walk.

"People are forgotten. Eventually no one remembers you."

Waterlily has immaculate skin, but is worried that she doesn't have beautiful enough knees. Should I tell her not

70

to worry about her knees? Men don't give any thought to knees, they don't think about women in parts, but in overall pictures. Do they do that? I think of my own intimate diaries.

Mom has already made arrangements regarding the flora on her grave. She wants to have low ivy, dwarf willow. Should I write: no pomp, no handles on the coffin, just the cheapest wooden box, raw?

I make a first draft of the letter and write: *I'm gone then.* Why *then?* Cross it out.

I add: *I won't be coming back.* Cross out *I won't be coming back* and write *I no longer exist.* Should I mention the spring? Where could that come in? Suddenly I'd like to insert the words "latter half" into the letter. Could I say: In the latter half of next week I will no longer exist? Or: In the latter half of next week the world will be spinning without me? What's the weather forecast for the world without me? They're forecasting mild weather and rain over the next few days. I write: *In the latter half of next week it will stop raining.* Waterlily will know what I mean.

Cross everything out.

Start again:

I don't think any real father could have been any prouder than I am. Cross out *real* and just leave *father.*

Rip up the sheet and start again:

Sold Steel Legs Ltd. to Eiríkur Gudmundsson (yes, it's the guy who runs the Steel Frame Ltd. company and makes kitchen

71

islands), he'll transfer the final payment to your account in June. Yours, Dad.

God saves the sufferers with suffering

I pack for a corpse. The suitcase is almost empty: no suncream, no razor, no change of shirt, no sandals, swimsuit, or shorts, no camera and no phone. It will be impossible to contact me.

Then I tidy up the apartment a bit.

I spread the duvet over the double bed and smoothen it slightly, then draw the bedspread over the bedclothes and tug on the corners on both sides to even them out. Should I vacuum as well? I open the wardrobe. Is that really the sweater Gudrún knitted for me, folded at the very back of the shelf?

I adjust the pile of books on the bedside table. What's the Bible still doing there? The bookmark is still on the Book of Job.

After Gudrún and I stopped sharing our nights together, and she lay on one side of the bed, wrapped in down with her book, and I lay on the other side with mine, I read three books that no one I know has managed to read from beginning to end: the Bible, the Koran, and the Vedas. It took me three months to read the Bible, a total of 1,829 pages, but a shorter time to read the others. My favourites were the love verses of the apostle Paul and the Koran's messages of peace. *For he who murders one man murders all mankind; he who saves a human life saves mankind.* And I liked Purusha in the Vedas with his *thousand heads, thousand eyes and thousand legs,* who held the entire world *in his embrace.*

Only on one occasion did Gudrún ask me to read to her. By then she was dressing our duvets in nonmatching covers and building a barricade of pillows between us, like a fortified wall between the east and west banks of the marital bed.

"Which part would you like me to read?" I asked.

"Just where you are now."

I was in the Book of Job so I read about the righteous Job, blameless and upright, God-fearing and scrupulous, who was imprisoned in chains and afflicted with suffering.

Naked came I out of my mother's womb, and naked shall I return, I end my reading.

"Thanks," she said softly, and I sensed a vulnerability in her voice. Then I heard her say, "I knew it," as she shook the pillow between us and turned away. I looked at her beautiful curved shoulder under her nightdress. If I had been on the Song of Songs and read *your breasts are like bunches of grapes* I'd probably still be a married man.

A short while later she had to go to the bathroom and when she came back, she said:

"The tap is leaking."

The next day there was a note on the kitchen table that read:

"A bulb blew in the hallway."

In this way we met halfway; I passed on suffering to her, she assigned me chores.

I could proclaim the world till dusk
There is something everywhere

When I've washed the plate, dried it, and put it back into the cupboard, I wipe the drainboard and hang the kitchen cloth.

I open all the windows.

I close all the windows.

Once I've finished making the double bed, I lie on the sofa for two hours and try to think of nothing. Is there anything, I ask myself, that can still surprise me in life? The evil of man? No, my knowledge of human cruelty is complete. Human kindness? No, I have met enough good men to believe in man. The immeasurable beauty of mountaintops, multiple layers of landscape, mountains behind mountains, multiple blues on blue? Endless black sand beaches and glistening glaciers in the east, the outline of a thousand-year dream that moves slowly, as if it were under a sheet of plexiglass? I know all that. Is there something I still long to experience? Nothing I can think of. I have held a newborn slimy red baby, chopped down a Christmas tree in the woods in December, taught a child to ride a bike, changed a tyre up on a mountain road alone at night in a snowstorm, plaited my daughter's hair, driven through a polluted valley full of factories abroad, rattled in the rear carriage of a small train, boiled potatoes on a Primus in a coal-black sand desert, wrestled with the truth under long and short shadows, and I know that a man both cries and laughs, that he suffers and loves, that he possesses a thumb and writes poems, and I know that a man knows that he is mortal.

What's left? To hear the chirp of a nightingale? To eat a white dove?

As the taxi waits outside, I turn back at the doorstep and fetch a few tools. There is no telling what circumstances I might land in, I might need to put up a hook. I also take an extension lead and transformer, which is when I realise I may as well take the small toolbox, the one with the rechargeable drill. Before shutting the door, I grab the photograph of Waterlily from the bedside table. She is five years old with a thin pigtail and swollen gums, having just lost her front teeth. The photograph was taken at a camping site by a lagoon on the tail of a glacier, and she is stretching five fingers up to the sky, with a turquoise iceberg in the background. As I pass the dustbins, it occurs to me that someone could dig my diaries out of the garbage and read my confessions, *Apologia pro Vita Sua*. The journals are clearly marked Jónas Ebeneser Snæland. Why do I identify myself with Mom's surname? I roll the notebooks together and stick them into my jacket pocket.

They'll go into the first trash can I find abroad.
I'm off then.
To a meeting with myself.
And my last day.
I say goodbye to everything.
The crocus have opened.
I leave nothing behind.
I move from the all-enveloping light into the darkness.

What is now
ends now

I doze off on the plane and dream of a sheep licking my ear and wake up just before landing.

The plane dives through the clouds.

I glide.

I glide.

I glide to the earth close to the salty sea.

I manage to make out a flat terrain, fields, endless forests, and dead-still lakes like mirrors in the landscape. The shadow of the steel wing stretches over a field to the edge of a forest. The runway embraces me at full speed; I've landed. Trees with foliage appear close to the windows. I peer out at the horizon, at the seam between the woods and the sky. This is where I'll go and no farther.

I give myself a week to finish the job.

I am a forest and a night of dark trees:
but he who is not afraid of my darkness,
will find banks full of roses

A man in a waist jacket stands by the exit holding up a
sheet of paper with two names: "Mister Jónas" has been
written with a red marker on the top of the page and
below it is a female name. We are the only two passengers
the hotel has come to collect and we share the back seat
of the taxi. The woman sits behind the driver, wearing
sunglasses despite the cloudy sky. It's a dusty old cab with
ripped upholstery, I feel the springs pressing against my
back, the seat belt is torn.

"Married" is the first word to come out of the cabbie's
mouth as he nods at us, first looking at me for confirmation,
and then at the woman, which is when I realise that it's a
question. The woman shakes her head and says something
to the driver in their language. She is in a blue jacket and
skirt with a foulard around her neck and she leans forward
slightly, holding onto the front seat as if she were posing for
a picture in a photo studio. I've never travelled far enough
from home not to be able to understand a single word that is
being spoken, never far enough not to be able to understand
the waiter who is handing me a beer, or he me.

Hotel Silence stands by the shore, an hour's drive from
the airport, but the driver explains that the roads are still
a mess and that we have to take a detour through the city,

which will prolong our journey by half an hour. Parts of the route haven't been mapped, he says. There are some hills in the distance, but otherwise the country is flat.

The first thing I notice is grey dust over everything, like a layer of ash after a volcanic eruption. Apart from the red streak stretching across the afternoon sky, we are driving into a black-and-white film set.

The driver confirms my feeling.

"Dust is the worst," he says. "Breathing in the dust. We are waiting for rain. Then it will all turn into mud, of course. The rain brings dampness too."

I notice he adjusts the mirror every time he addresses us, to have us both in view. He drives with his right hand, while his left hand lies motionless in his lap. When he is pointing at something, he takes his hand off the wheel altogether and the car swerves on the road.

I spot the fragment of an old town wall.

"Once there were ancient Roman ruins here, now it's just ordinary ruins," I hear him say. "It will take us fifty years to build up the country again. The refugees won't come back while things are still a mess," he continues. "And we don't get tourists anymore. We are no longer on the news. We are forgotten. We no longer exist."

He says the hotel was closed for many months and that it's quite significant that he's now driven three guests there in the same week. That's in total, including us, he says, holding up three fingers and the car swerves.

We don't pass a single undamaged building. The man points and provides commentary: the House of Parliament was destroyed, as were the museum and the TV station, which are in ruins, the National Archive and its manuscripts was also razed to the ground, and the Museum of Modern Art was blown up. "Here there used to be a school, there a library, there a university, here there was a bakery, here a cinema," he continues.

Destruction lies everywhere.

High apartment blocks have been blown apart and there is an obvious shortage of glass in the windows of the walls that are still standing. I think to myself: You have your derelict, crumbling houses, we have our boulders that crack open with molten rock flowing through them like streams.

We slowly meander through the city, the few people about look pale and weary. In some places machinery is working in the ruins. There are widespread traces of the prosperity people enjoyed before the war. We stop at a crossroads, just beside a two-storey house with a missing facade, like a dollhouse. Although everything is covered in a thick layer of dust, I distinguish a patterned carpet on the floor and the remains of a piano. I'm transfixed by a deep armchair and footrest by a famous designer. Beside the armchair there is a lampstand and an overturned bookshelf. I notice the bed has been made in the room, someone has drawn a white blanket over the double bed just before abandoning the house, perhaps the person popped out to the bakery for some buns and got shot on the way. What draws my attention the most, though, is an unbroken yellow vase on a shelf in the living room. The wreck of a station wagon lies in the garage and a red tricycle stands in the driveway.

Garbage is scattered everywhere and, as far as I can make out, the sewage pipes have been unearthed. The driver apologises that it is impossible to wind up the window on my side. Apart from the pungent smell from outside and the strong odour of the driver's Fahrenheit aftershave, I catch a faint, sweet flowery scent from the woman, totally different than Gudrún's. What was the name of that perfume she wore again? Wasn't she the companion of stars, with *Pluto* behind her ears? The woman silently stares at the road between the front seats.

"Developers," says the driver, nodding towards some giant Caterpillar excavators. "After the air raids, the peace-keeping forces arrived," he continues. "Then they and the contractors started showing up with their machinery." He takes his hand off the wheel to adjust the mirror yet again. His eyes are now aimed at me.

He wants to know what I'm doing in this place.

"Vacation," I say.

They both stare at me, the man and the woman. I notice them exchanging a glance in the mirror. The man says something I don't understand to the woman, then they look at me again and nod. I observe them.

He rephrases his question and asks if I'm on a *special mission*, like the man he had driven to the hotel earlier in the week.

I repeat that I'm on vacation and they ask no more questions.

We move away from the city, driving up twisted country roads with woodlands on both sides. I notice that the tree trunks are grey, it's as if a large part of the trees in the forest have been unable to leaf or flower.

On the outskirts of the forest there is a field where the driver slows down, lifting his hand from the wheel to point, causing the car to zigzag along the road.

"Graves, unmarked mass graves," he says, including a famous national poet who wrote a poem about a desolate forest.

The woman says something and I sense the driver's unease in his seat.

He shakes his head.

The woman addresses me for the first time.

"Here people have buried sons, husbands, and fathers," says the woman. "In many places fathers lie with sons, side by side, even three generations of men from the same family." She says that war broke out between houses, between neighbours whose children were in school together, between work colleagues, between members of the chess club, between strikers and goalies on the soccer team. "On one side there was the family doctor," she rattles off impassively, "on the other the plumber and singing teacher. Former choir members turned into enemies, the baritone on one side, the bass and tenor on the other."

She falls silent and gazes out the window.

I wonder what the cabbie did to survive. Why isn't he buried on the outskirts of the woods? Was he an executioner or a victim? Is he perhaps responsible for some freshly dug graves of fathers and sons? He is silent and seems to be concentrating on his driving.

Shortly afterwards he starts talking again, but switches topics and says that before the war he drove various big stars to the health spa hotel, as he calls it.

"Specially to rest and improve health."

He reflects a moment.

"Like Mick Jagger, for example. The funny thing was," he continues, "that they were playing 'I Can't Get No Satisfaction' on the radio at the same time. But he didn't sing along. Jagger I mean."

He's silent before picking up the thread again:

"If it wasn't him, it was someone very like him. With one eye brown and the other blue."

"Could it have been David Bowie?" I ask. They both look at me and the man gives it some thought.

"Yes, now that you say it, it could have been David Bowie."

Now that he recalls it better, the driver thinks it might have been the song about a waiting starman in the sky that they were listening to, he and his passenger.

"But he was shorter than I expected him to be," he continues. Which didn't surprise him because he had heard that famous people are smaller than you think. "People are either taller or shorter than you expect," he adds.

And while the driver was watching Mick Jagger or David Bowie through the rearview mirror, he noticed how he was moving his big lips to the song.

"That sounds like Jagger," I say.

He nods.

"Yeah, I'm sure it was one of the two."

The woman smiles. Is she smiling at me?

Dusk is falling as we drive into the town under the bloody sky. The streets are narrow and cobbled and the car meanders on. My gaze shifts to a paved lane and I notice that there are large holes in the exposed pipes like flayed flesh.

As the driver is taking the suitcases out of the boot I notice that his left jacket sleeve, which had lain motionless in his lap, is empty.

He raises the stump.

"Land mine," he says, and adds that he was lucky because he got away with losing his hearing in one ear and half an arm.

"It makes all the difference to have kept my elbow."

Then he moves the hair off one ear with his whole hand and shows me the half-ear and the scar that stretches to his temple.

"The rearview mirror helps me to understand what people are saying. I look and then I *hear*," he adds.

And me I think: I hear and see.

As I'm walking through the entrance of Hotel Silence holding my toolbox, I hear him say:

"You think air raids solve everything." Although more to himself.

II

SCARS

Watching over everything is the silence, silence

Although Hotel Silence has clearly pulled through the war reasonably unscathed, it still leaves a lot to be desired when compared to its online photographs. It's as if all of its colours have faded, like a pale body that hasn't seen the sun for a long time. A musty scent lingers in the air. I recognise the chandeliers on the ceiling but their light is dull and grey and lacks sparkle.

The young man at the reception desk speaks English, like the driver, and could be about twenty years old, the same age I was when I started keeping a diary about cloud formations and the flesh. He's in a white shirt and tie and sports a long fringe, which every now and then he strokes to one side.

We stand side by side for a very brief moment, the woman and I, like a couple checking into a hotel, then I take one step back with my toolbox. As the woman is filling out a form, I glance around. She and the young man talk in hushed tones.

I immediately see that the hotel needs maintenance. In many places the paint is peeling and the ceiling shows signs of both dampness and damaged plaster. I wouldn't be surprised if the building hasn't been heated for a long time, it is not unlike returning to a cold summer house in the spring after a winter of heavy snow. This place should be aired and patched up here and there. I knock on the wall but can't identify the type of wood. What kind of forests were we driving through? Redwood? The entrance hall also serves as a kind of lobby and what draws my attention is the large fireplace. It has been lit and the smell of smoke wafts through the air.

Above the fire there is a painting of a forest, in the middle of which stands a leopard who gazes out of the picture while a hunter stares at the beast with a fearless glint in his eyes. The wild animal, though, looks like a fairly harmless feline with doll's eyes.

I notice the young man occasionally peeping at me as he attends to the woman. She doesn't remove her sunglasses, so it occurs to me that she might have a migraine after her journey.

Once the woman has vanished up the stairs with a key, the young man turns to me and leans over the desk, confidentially:

"Movie star."

He seems to be wracking his brain.

"What was the last movie she starred in again?" He thinks a moment. "*Man with a Mission*? No," he corrects himself. "Wasn't it *Man without a Mission*?"

But then he's not sure anymore and says she hasn't been seen here on a big screen for a while.

I'm asked to fill out several forms, which takes up con-siderable time, the questionnaire is similar to the one at the airport. Parents. Where were they born? Should I write Laxárdalur in the eastern district of Húnavatn in Mom's column? Family status, children, next of kin, emergency number? Who should be called in the event of a mishap? I write Gudrún Waterlily Jónasdóttir and her phone number. He runs through the form to make sure I've filled in all the boxes.

"They ask for your height," he says, pointing at the page.

I write one metre eighty-five.

That should be useful when they're making a box for me.

"I would have guessed one eighty-three," says the young man.

He apologises for the paperwork, regulations that have to be followed. We're alone, but he lowers his voice nonetheless and swiftly looks around.

"We want to know what people are doing in the country."

He explains that this isn't a big hotel, sixteen bedrooms in all, and only five being used at the moment.

He then confirms what the cabdriver had said about the hotel having had no guests for many months and then suddenly three in the same week.

"You, the lady, and the man," he says, before adding that they heated my room earlier in the day.

Next he unfolds a map and leans over it with a blue pen. He crosses out different areas, saying: ruins, gone. He then gets a red pen and draws circles on the map, saying land mines. Here and here. And here. Don't go into the woods, don't wander into fields. Avoid deserted areas. "Don't step on anything here, here, here, and here," he says. "Don't go there or there. Or here. Don't pick mushrooms. Plastic mines are dangerous because detectors can't find them."

He hands me the key.

"You're in number seven." And adds:

"There is a curfew from eleven at night till six in the morning. Electricity is rationed and power is cut for six hours every day. Water is also rationed. If you want to take a shower, it has to be before nine in the morning, after that hot water is finished. And don't be longer in the shower than three minutes, otherwise my sister has no shower."

I don't ask him why his sister needs to shower in the hotel, but he volunteers an explanation regardless:

"She works at the hotel, like me."

He hesitates.

"In fact, you could say we pretty much run it."

He peers at the forms.

"It says here you are staying for a week. The dining room is still closed, but we serve breakfast. There is also a restaurant down the road that is open if we let them know you are coming."

And another thing, if I need him I should ring the bell. But he is not always at the desk, because he is also busy with other tasks.

When I booked the hotel online, there was some mention of ancient baths and a famous mosaic mural that were discovered when they were digging the foundations of the building, if I remember correctly.

I ask the young man about the mural, whether it's accessible.

"I would love to see it," I add. Suddenly the young man no longer understands English.

"It's connected to the hotel, is it not?" And I add—in an effort to jog his memory—that the subject of the mosaic is nude women.

What had really attracted my attention, though, was the strange turquoise colour of the background, which was said to be attributable to an old stone quarry in the country. Unfortunately the young man is not aware of the existence of this mosaic or any other ancient ruins in the area. There must be some misunderstanding, he says, suddenly busying himself with the paperwork on the desk. It seems to be just two sheets.

"I'm sorry," he says.

And is he not familiar with the ancient thermal baths in the hotel either? The mud baths?

No, he has no recollection of them, but says he'll make enquiries.

As I'm walking up the stairs I hear the young man say without looking up:

"Yes, and the lift is broken."

On my way to the room it occurs to me that from now on I don't have to say any more words than I want to, that I could shut up until the end of the world.

Reached this precise point in life
in room number seven

The first thing I notice when I turn the key in the lock and switch on the light is the painting over the bed. It's not unlike the forest picture in the lobby, except that instead of a leopard it's a lion and, instead of the wild animal gazing out of the painting, the hunter and the animal are looking each other in the eye.

The leafy wallpaper in the room is starting to peel in the corners.

The room contains a desk and an armchair with carved legs and woven upholstery. A fresh bar of soap on the sink, wrapped in thin silk paper adorned with flowers, gives off an old Lux-like scent. The bedspread is covered with dust but the sheets underneath are clean.

I lie on the bedspread in my clothes and turn on the bedside lamp. The bulb flickers a few times and then dies. I glance at my watch and see that there's another hour before the power is cut off, so I fetch my screwdriver and torch and place them beside the lamp.

I feel cold after the journey.

I open the suitcase and arrange my belongings on the table, side by side. That doesn't take long. I hang my red shirt in the wardrobe and place my sweater on the shelf beside it, and I keep my diaries on the table beside my toolbox. I haven't come across a garbage can in this country yet. I have practically nothing. Nine things.

Should I go to bed, should I brush my teeth?

I unscrew the tap. At first it spurts sand, then a brown muddy liquid, and finally red water. The water is cold and without enough pressure to be able to take a shower. The noise from the pipes suggests they need to be examined.

Creaking can be heard from the bed on the other side of the wall, someone is tossing and turning sleeplessly in the room next door, unless it's the two of them, the woman and the other man, and they're rubbing their sweaty bodies against each other. Is that a child's voice I just heard? Is someone singing a lullaby?

There is a slit between the blinds and outside the world is engulfed in total darkness. I hear the sound of a scooter being started and a buzz, which it occurs to me might be the singing of crickets. All of a sudden I think I hear rustling outside my door and then as if something were gently scratching it, from below. Finally, not a single other sound is heard.

The only thing that keeps me awake is my own heartbeat under the water lily.

Boom, boom, boom.

It won't be long now, though, before dead stillness reigns in my chest.

It's cold on top of the bedspread and it's cold under the sheets and, at some stage in the night, I grope through the darkness to get my sweater in the wardrobe—I don't expect to find a down quilt. As soon as I open the wardrobe door it comes off in my arms. I grab the torch and examine the joints, it would seem that the hinges were being held up by a total of two loose screws. I should have a box with the right screws and will fix it tomorrow. I put on the sweater Gudrún knitted for me and curl up under the sheets, a forty-nine-year-old foetus, isn't it logical that I think of Mom?

I turn the torch back on and reach for one of the notebooks that I open at random.

At the top of a page in the middle of the book I've written the following in wavy blue handwriting: *The human heart beats seventy times per minute. The bigger the creature is, the slower the heartbeat. An elephant's heart beats twenty-three times per minute. Once a heart has beaten a certain number of times, it stops.*

Under his wings you will find refuge

I wake up to a giant bird running in circles around the room, strenuously flapping its wings up and down, as if it were trying to take off in flight, but then he shoots through the door as quick as a flash and silently closes it behind him.

It's a child.

Didn't I lock the door? The lock is old, it might have jammed.

I takes me a few moments to remember what part of the globe I've landed in. I try to guess the time from the light filtering under the curtains and look at my watch. I've slept for ten hours and still have words from my dreams hanging on my lips. It's Mom talking to me:

"Instead of putting an end to your existence, can't you put an end to you being you and just become someone else?"

A short while later there is a knock on the door and a young woman appears on the threshold. She is wearing a white polo neck and skirt and might be the same age as Waterlily. I expect it's the sister mentioned by the young man in reception and the thought flashes through my mind that she will probably be the one to discover me and inform her brother in the lobby, who will then call the police.

The woman apologises for the disturbance and asks when I would like her to make the bed and whether I need anything. A clean towel? The hot water ration is actually finished for the day. It's obvious that I've slept in my clothes and she scrutinises me. I also notice her scanning the room. The toolbox is open on the bedside table but her gaze freezes on the loose door leaning against the wardrobe.

I stand up and say I'll fix the door.

"I'll take care of it." Yes, that's how I put it.

She watches me fetch the drill and box of screws and tells me that her brother had told her I was on vacation. I sense it's really a question, the bit about me being on vacation. She looks at me, waiting for me to counter her assertion.

"Yes, that's right, I'm on vacation."

"Not much luggage, mister?"

I explain to her that I'm only making a short stop.

"I won't be long," I say.

In fact, it's written in black and white on the booking that I'll be staying for a week.

I notice the curiosity in her expression and expect her to ask me what I'm doing with a drill on vacation. She doesn't. Instead she repeats what her brother said the day before, that it's kind of weird that they haven't had guests for many months and then suddenly three in the same week.

"So we hope the truce will last and that tourists will come back again. We need currency," she adds.

She stands watching me as I screw the door back into place. That's quickly done. She tests the door with one hand and eagerly thanks me.

The shirt I came with hangs on a wooden hanger inside the wardrobe.

The door to the corridor is open and a brief moment

later a short being appears. It's a boy. He shoots past the woman with a towel tied around his shoulders, which he uses as a cape, and runs one circle around the room before vanishing again through the door, down the corridor.

I sense her becoming insecure and she says something to the boy as he whizzes away.

"He's flying," she says apologetically. "He doesn't play with the other children."

Could this be her own child she's brought to work? When it comes to it—once I've chosen the day—I'll tell her she can't bring the boy in. Let's say Tuesday of next week. I could decide it here and now and it will be Tuesday of next week.

I grab the opportunity and ask her straight-out:

"Your son?"

She nods and says the kindergarten is still closed, but that he should be starting school in the autumn.

"If they've finished fixing the building," she says, adding that she can't bear the thought of leaving the child on his own, nor allowing him to play outside because he could wander into an area of land mines. Some are to be found in football pitches and playgrounds.

Not only do the young siblings have to run Hotel Silence, they also have to take care of a child.

"We came here towards the end of the war," she continues. This was the last stop. After this town it was just the

97

ocean, she adds, and as she is talking, she tries opening and closing the wardrobe door several times.

"If it is possible to talk about ending up somewhere," she says, as if she were addressing the wardrobe.

"And are you and your brother the owners of the hotel?"

She hesitates.

"No, our auntie. She's actually left the country. You could say we run it for her."

Then she's about to add something but holds back.

I feel the need to fully understand:

"And you live here with the boy, you and your brother? In the hotel?"

She nods and says they're waiting for a house in the town. The house she intends to move into—along with some other women and her son and brother—was damaged and has no water or electricity.

"Meanwhile, we live here," she says, and disappears into the bathroom to place some towels. I hear her unscrew the tap.

"The water is clear," she says in amazement. She is standing in the doorway.

"There's no more sand," she adds.

"I cleared the pipes."

I hear her turning on the shower.

"The shower works too. And the water is hot," she says from inside the bathroom.

She's astonished.

"Yes, I just had to unscrew the showerhead and clear out the sand and mud inside it."

Then she's suddenly at the window and has drawn up the blind.

"We used to come here on our holidays as children, my brother and I," I hear her say.

She stands silently by the window a moment, with her back turned to me.

"There," she then says, pointing out the window. "Against that wall people were shot. There was a bakery beside it and it was difficult to avoid that corner."

I approach the window.

"There?"

"Yes. The bullet holes can still be seen in the wall. Anywhere people formed a group or a line there was the risk of being shot." And she explains that there were battles between neighbourhoods and there was a state of siege, so that some districts were isolated for months on end.

"The people survived by passing food through a tunnel," she adds.

I think about this. Looking from the window it's difficult to work out where the sniper might have been positioned.

She becomes silent but then continues:

"There are a number of theories on who the shooter was." She hesitates and looks over her shoulder, as if trying to ensure that no one is standing at the door.

Unless she is checking on the boy.

"I've heard it's a member of the choir," she says, adjusting the elastic in her hair.

All over the city
I am buried

Apart from fixing the wardrobe door there are no other chores on the list today. No one knows about me and no one is expecting me. I know that my mother, beyond the ice-cold ocean, is listening to the afternoon story on the radio and eating her rhubarb pudding with cream, but no one expects anything from me. I haven't been jobless for twenty-six years. What am I to do with a whole six days? Excluding seven hours of sleep, that leaves me with seventeen hours a day to be filled.

"Seventeen times six equals a hundred and two hours," Mom would have immediately answered.

That means that the glowing star will rise above the earth's horizon six more times.

Is there still something I want to do?

I could go sightseeing, particularly since I've now repeated the claim that I'm on vacation ten times. What church, what museum, what archaeological sites should I visit?

Yesterday the brother at the reception desk had no recollection of the existence of a mosaic mural or other relics, maybe he'll remember them today.

I ring the bell twice, it takes the young man ten minutes to appear. When he finally does, he is busy doing up the buttons of his white shirt. I notice he is wearing tracksuit trousers and plimsolls and has dust and grey particles in his hair that look like plaster or putty, as if he had been working with cement. He has headphones around his neck, which he takes off and places on the desk without turning off Lorde.

I ask him about the mosaic mural again:

"Have you found out anything about that mural? The antiquities?"

"No, unfortunately," he says. "It takes a long time. I'm working on it."

I give him more clues and tell him that, according to the information I found online—to be more precise, on Hotel Silence's website—the wall is divided in two. One part dates back to antiquity, while the other is a more recent addition connected to the health spa the hotel advertises.

"You can't rely on everything you see on the Web," says the young man. "Besides, that was before the war," he explains. "A lot has changed since then." He then thanks me for reminding him to update the website.

"I'll continue to make enquiries and will let you know if I find anything," he adds, focusing his attention on adjusting the stack of maps on the counter.

He then wants to know where I'm off to.

"Going on a walk."

Then, as quick as a flash, he unfolds a map of the town and repeats yesterday's instructions on the places I shouldn't set foot if I don't want to be reduced to a maimed trunk; not here and absolutely not here. And once again he warns me about deserted areas.

"The sun also shines on the surface of graves," he concludes, folding the map again. And because I have slept through breakfast, he recommends the only open restaurant down the road. If I want, he can call the owner and let him know to expect me. That way I could be sure he's cooked something.

I suddenly realise that the young man could be my son's age, that is to say if I had managed to create another living being.

You who I cross upon

Here I am down on the earth.

Literally speaking.

I spread out the map of the town square. The weather is still and warm and the air is golden with dust.

In the square there is a flock of grey pigeons. I remember what the cabdriver said yesterday:

"Even the birds vanished in the war."

Machinery can be heard in the distance, some construction is being done in the town. I meander down narrow streets and feel like I'm always turning at the same corner. Some of the houses look intact, but others were clearly abandoned in haste. There aren't many people about, but in some odd way many of the faces look strangely familiar. There's a woman who looks like my ex-sister-in-law, Gudrún's sister, and for a moment I think I catch a glimpse of Svanur's back. I scrutinise the people but they don't look back at me. Many of them are missing an arm or a leg or some other body part that others normally possess as a pair.

Then I remember when Gudrún asked me out of the blue whether I would donate her a kidney if she ever needed one. I said yes and asked if she was ill, but she said no. I thought, what if she asks about my heart? Would I then tell her that I'll gladly give her anything that I have more than one of?

"Those are the kind of questions women ask," Svanur would have said. "A sign of them putting you to the test."

Ultimately, I must reach the wall peppered with bullet holes. Sure enough, I reach the wall that faces my hotel-room window and examine it up close, standing in the very footsteps of those unsuspecting people shot at on some afternoon or starlit night. I stroke the lukewarm stone, slipping my fingers into the bullet holes.

"People dream simple dreams," Svanur would say. "To avoid getting pointlessly shot and hoping your children will remember you." Judging by the density of the holes,

103

it does not seem unlikely that executions happened here. But the cabdriver had said they were carried out in the football fields.

The hotel is in my direct line of view, and when I focus my gaze on the second floor, where my bedroom window is, for a moment I get the feeling that someone is standing behind the glass and observing me, someone who turns on the light and then turns it off just as swiftly again, as if playing with the switch or sending important Morse code messages to the town: *No More Games. No More Bombs. No More Walking.*

Time is full of dead cats

Since I'm not dying today, I need to eat.

It isn't difficult to find Restaurant Limbo, which the young man pointed out to me on the map. It's located on the main street between the town's hair salon, which is closed—although two hairdresser's chairs and a large photograph of a young Sophia Loren are on display in the window—and a children's boutique, which is also closed, like most of the other stores on the street. I try to decipher the signs in the windows to understand what was housed where. Some of the brand names are international and I recognise a poster of a well-known brand hanging inside a shuttered shop window: "Life is short, let's buy jeans." Opposite the restaurant there is another children's clothing store, and beside that a sign reads Pizza Verona and another reads Café Amsterdam, both places deserted and closed. On my way I pass a boarded-up cinema displaying a poster of Bruce Willis, with bulging biceps and soot on his forehead, in a broken display case by the entrance.

The red curtains in the windows of Restaurant Limbo are drawn, so it's impossible to see inside, but as soon as I approach, the doors open wide.

The man who escorts me to a table by the window tells me they phoned from the hotel to let them know I was on my way, so that the "dish of the day" is already in the oven.

He places a handwritten sheet marked "Dish of the Day" in front of me with no further clarification and a ridiculously low price beside it. I realise that I could survive several weeks in this country on the money I exchanged at the airport.

"Very good," says the man.

He places a fork, a glass, and a cloth napkin on the table and gets me a beer. "Neptunus," the label reads on the bottle.

I'm the only customer in the place.

"You won't be disappointed," he adds. "Speciality." I wait half an hour for the food while the man chats with me, an apron tied around his neck and a tea towel tossed over his shoulder. He wants to know what I'm doing in town and, like the cabdriver, asks if I'm on a special mission.

I tell him I'm on vacation and by way of emphasis point a finger at the map of the town I have spread out on the table.

He wants to know where I'm from and whether there have been any recent wars there.

"Not since 1238," I say.

"So you didn't participate in the air raids?"

"No, we don't have an army."

He then says that he's heard that I fixed a wardrobe door at the hotel this morning.

"That kind of news spreads fast," he says, and I notice he is wearing impeccably polished, elegant black shoes, like many of the men I have seen on my walk.

He doesn't wait for any confirmation, but instead informs me of what the young man at the hotel has already shared, that the hotel is owned by the aunt of the siblings who run it. That she—that is to say, the aunt—is a widow who inherited the hotel from one of her husband's relatives and that she has left the country.

"Many people died in the war and so it is not always clear who owns what."

I notice a curled-up cat in a corner of the room. He's the first four-legged creature I've encountered in this town. When the man moves away to fetch my food, the cat stands and coils itself at my feet. As I bend down to pet the animal, I get the feeling I've seen this striped grey cat with a black muzzle before. He looks like a female cat I've sometimes petted on my street at home; it all fits, same bone structure, same fur, same bushy tail.

"There weren't many animals left in town at the end of the war," says the owner when he returns, nodding towards the kitten. And then adds: "The meat is not unlike rabbit meat."

He places the dish in front of me and even though it's quite dark inside the restaurant, I see from the shape and bone structure of the roast that it's the meat of some small animal. He makes a separate trip to fetch a knife and turns the handle of the razor-sharp blade towards me as he passes it.

A knife can be used to slice bread just as easily as a man's throat, I think to myself.

I'm a man who is not fussy about food and eats anything that is put in front of me when I'm hungry. I occasionally used to buy a hot dog on my way home from work and don't cook elaborate meals, but rather buy chops in breadcrumbs and fry them with *Season-All* and eat them straight off the pan as soon as they're ready, standing over the cooker.

It occurs to me that the meal might be a bird and I try to remember what migrant birds stop in these parts before setting across the turbulent grey ocean to build a nest on a heath between two tussocks on a bright spring island. The owner, who has positioned himself by the edge of the table to watch me debone the meat, confirms my suspicions.

"Pigeon," he says.

107

It all makes sense, he got the contents of the menu from the street.

"Not a white one, actually," he adds. "We don't have all the ingredients that we want."

The dish comes as a surprise and turns out to be tasty.

I ask about the spice and the owner lights up with interest.

"Cumin" is the answer. "Very good?" he says, simultaneously nodding his head to indicate that this is both a question and an affirmation. The recipe was supposed to include mushrooms, but they have been removed from the menu since it is too dangerous to pick them.

The owner stands over me and waits for me to put my cutlery down beside the carcass of the bird, so that he can take the plate away. He scurries into the kitchen and swiftly returns, coffee is on its way. He places two cups on the table and two tumblers, drags over a chair from the next table, and sits opposite me to chat some more. The coffee is strong, as is the schnapps, but both are good. Despite being alone in the establishment, he quickly glances over his shoulder, lowers his voice, and says he's heard I travel with a drill.

"Yes, and we heard that you checked out the pipes at Hotel Silence."

I don't ask who's "we."

"No, the fact is," he says, finishing his coffee and downing his tumbler in one gulp, "that I wanted to ask if you might be able to help me make a door."

I tell him I'm on vacation—it's the third time I mention it.

The man continues regardless and says he wants to change the entrance into the restaurant, to have a door on hinges that will open both in and out.

"And so that it will be possible to see who is coming in," he adds.

Before I manage to protest any further, he has pulled out a folded sheet of paper from his breast pocket, which he unfolds and smoothes out with the palms of his hands. He lays it out on the table in front of me.

"With wings. Swinging doors," he says, pointing at his amateurish pencil drawing.

Judging by the sketch, the doors are to be on hinges and curved in shape. He has put a lot of work into the curves and used a rubber unsparingly.

"Yes, like in the Wild West," I say.

The man sitting opposite me has the expression of one who has finally met a person who understands him. He nods.

"You got it. John Wayne. The *invincible* one."

I tell him I'm no carpenter and that, apart from anything else, I don't have the right tools and prepare to stand.

"No problem," he answers. "You're a handyman and I'll get the tools for you."

He shakes his head when I pull out my wallet with the intention of paying. Instead he wants to know if I'll take a look at his pipes for him. In the kitchen.

"Later," I say.

"Yes, next time," he says.

He follows me to the door, as does the cat who stands up when I do. It is then that I realise that one of the cat's eyes is shut, that it's a one-eyed cat. I bend over to stroke its fur.

"Cats have always outlived man," he says. "If not your cat, then someone else's."

The man stands in the doorway and points at a sign in a dark window across the road. I'd noticed similar signs all over town: "Room to Let."

"Most houses rent rooms to tourists. We hope things are picking up again. Yesterday the other foreigner in the hotel came to eat and today you, so we have every reason to be optimistic."

An urge to touch a woman

When I get back to the hotel, the movie star is standing at the reception desk talking to the young man. They both suddenly fall silent as I enter.

She turns and greets me.

I find this difficult to explain, but I'm suddenly overcome by an urge to touch the woman, to caress her lower back, a feeling somewhere between stroking a cat and a newly smoothened wall. It is immediately followed by another feeling, like looking forward to calm weather or a spring that doesn't arrive—not at the time or in the manner one expects.

"I'm still trying to find out about that mosaic mural,"

says the young man hurriedly and turns his attention back to the woman again. He mutters something to her in hushed tones and I sense he's explaining something to do with me, because she swirls around and looks at me, and then nods at him approvingly.

On the way down the corridor to my room I hear someone calling me—a man of my age, standing in his doorway in a white dressing gown and leopard print socks and thick, hairy calves protruding in between. The belt of the dressing gown dangles loosely at his waist. I deduce this must be the other foreigner.

He is holding a bottle of light yellow liquid in one hand and a toothbrush glass in the other and wants to invite me in for a drink.

"No, thank you," I say, adding that I'm on my way to my room.

As soon as I say this, I realise it doesn't sound like a sufficiently pressing errand because he says: "Are you in such a hurry? We could also play a round of chess. Do you know Tal's attack strategy?"

He waves the bottle and takes one step down the narrow corridor, leaning one hand against the opposite wall, effectively blocking my path.

He says he heard a drill in the next room and has drawn the conclusion that I am working on the building.

I tell him I'm on vacation.

It delights him as if I'd hit the nail on the head.

He rephrases his question and wants to know who I'm working for.

I reflect on the question.

"No one. Myself," I add.

"Who sent you? Williams?"

"No."

"You must have some plan of action. Everyone has a plan. Business is all about focus."

He lowers his voice and looks around. The corridor bends at the corner and for a moment I think I see a small being dashing past the end of the passageway, and that it's naked, a little pale body that then vanishes in a flash, like a lizard fleeing the light.

"No one comes here without a mission. The best opportunities are now, the community is weak, lacks structure, and you can strike good deals. My friend is buying land and buildings."

I can almost hear Mom's voice: "War is a gold mine."

The man stands in front of me, pours some liquid out of the bottle into the toothbrush glass, and empties it.

I slip past him.

"Ever since I was a kid I've longed to kill someone," I hear him say behind me. "The only way to do that legally was to join the army. When I was nineteen years old, the dream came true."

I'm expecting him to ask me if I've tried killing. I would then tell him that I've fished trout.

Instead he says:

"You've got to create a system that the enemy doesn't understand. That's warfare. That's beauty. That's how Tal thought, leading his team to victory by sacrificing one man after the next."

MAY

The first thing I notice when I stick the key into the lock and open the door is the pool of water on the floor and, next to it, the boy sitting on a chair, wrapped in a towel with his toes dangling out. His mother is busy changing the bedclothes, the sheets are crumpled and the pillow lies on the floor. I notice that she has wet hair. My nine items have been rearranged on the table, in a straight line, like a train, one carriage after another. When the boy sees me, he covers his ears.

"I'm sorry" is the first thing the girl says. "After you fixed the pipes, this is the only shower that works. There is so little pressure in the water in our room. Just a few drops. I used the opportunity while you were away."

By "our" she is clearly referring to herself and the boy.

She says the boy ran out of the shower, which explains the puddle on the floor. Adam had then crawled up on the bed.

So the boy's name is Adam.

"He was so happy," she says as she picks up the wet towels.

The boy observes us but still keeps his hands over his ears.

She apologises again and says she should have asked me for permission. I tell her not to worry and that I'll take a look at the pipes in their room.

She says she actually intended to offer to switch rooms and move me to the other side of the corridor. In fact, she's already getting the room ready.

"That way you don't have to look down on the bullet-pocked street and you can have a view of the beach just like me and Adam."

The only issue is the shower in the bathroom, but she was wondering if I could take a look at the pipes. "To see the problem" is how she puts it.

After leaving with the child in her arms, enveloped in a towel, and going up to their room on the floor above, she reappears again. I see she has wound her wet hair into some kind of bun and tied it with an elastic the way Waterlily does sometimes.

It doesn't take me long to reassemble my earthly possessions—nine items—and I follow her into the new bedroom.

She has put clean sheets on the bed and opened the blinds and says that Fifi helped her move the desk in.

"I see you write," she adds, carefully scrutinizing me.

I assume Fifi must be her brother and imagine she is referring to the diaries.

A forest landscape painting hangs over the bed, not unlike those that hang in the other bedroom and the lobby, green boughs, green shadows, and a greenish sky. I notice that in the middle of the painting there is a cluster of light and in the middle of the light stands a leopard.

I step closer to examine the painting.

"Yes, there is one painting in each bedroom," she explains, positioning herself in front of the picture.

I sense they've all been painted by the same hand, since it transpires that they are all initialled with the letters "AD" in the bottom right-hand corner. She says she doesn't know the identity of the artist but has heard that the theme is the local forest.

"Before the war the painters around here painted trees and poets wrote about perfumed forests and transparent leaves rustling in the wind," she says expressionlessly.

Then she takes a deep breath.

"Now this same forest is a death trap. Full of land mines. Those who dare to go there don't see any leaves growing on the trees. Instead of cutting firewood, people prefer to rip up their parquets to heat their houses."

She takes a breath.

"Why should one want to venture into the woods?" I hear her say in a low voice. "Not to pick pinecones."

My new bedroom has a small balcony and a stairwell that looks like a fire escape and leads down into the backyard of the hotel. She points out the window and says that

115

the garden has been swept for mines, but nevertheless she recommends that I stick to the path if I'm going down to the beach.

"There used to be a golf course once, but it was dug up in the war to plant vegetables."

We stand side by side at the window observing the arid vegetation.

"I remember the smell of grass before the war," she continues, "and all kinds of berries: blackberries, raspberries, strawberries."

She hesitates.

"Then it was replaced by the smell of burning rubber, melted metal, dust, and blood. Especially blood."

She is silent but then continues.

"The first summer of the war was the most difficult, that the sun should be shining, birds chirping, and flowers sprouting out of the cold earth, and bombs exploding. One didn't expect it."

I say nothing.

"We're hoping for rain," she says finally. "It hasn't rained for two months and the land is parched."

We both slip into silence, she is still standing by the window.

Should I tell this young lady who dreams of hearing the pitter-patter of rain in a tin bucket that soon something green will grow here again, out of the dust, just wait and see? I could even quote the "Somnambulist Ballad" by the poet who was shot and buried in some unknown place, and say that here something green will grow, *Green green I want you green*, wouldn't that upset her? And add that the poet believed that a better country awaits us, bright beyond the edge of the sea. It also occurs to me to tell her that my sheep-farmer uncle and his young farmhands have burnt the withered grass every spring and left the scorched earth, black stumps that prickled out of the ground and smouldered for weeks on end after the flames licked the moss and heather, but ultimately it was overgrown in grass again, so good and green.

"We don't understand why we haven't had any spring thaw this year," I hear her say.

The cabdriver said the same.

"We are waiting for rain," he'd said as he shifted gears with his steering hand and the car swerved over to the other side of the road. "And when it starts to rain," he continued, "the river rises by about six metres and flows over the fields where the bodies lie, and skeletons in uniforms rise out of bottomless lakes. Then we will finally be able to bury the dead."

She suddenly approaches me with an outstretched hand. It's time for introductions.

"May."

I hold out my hand in return.

"Jónas."

Our relationship has become personal now.

117

That means I can no longer impose myself on her by killing myself on her watch.

ADAM

The mother and son's room is number fourteen on the second floor. Like the other hotel rooms, there are few personal items there, apart from some toys. The boy is in his pyjamas, with water-combed hair, sitting at the table eating an apple that has been sliced into pieces. He feigns not to see me. On the floor there is a row of little plastic men he has arranged one behind the other, with equal gaps, not unlike my tools on the table.

The mother and son clearly share the same bed, a stuffed rabbit lies on a pillow adorned with pictures of puppies.

"We fled with virtually no belongings, running from one place to another," she says when she sees me scanning the room. "Adam was born at the beginning of the war and has never had a home."

She follows me into the bathroom with the wrench and stands beside me as I clean the pipes. I also have a roll of black insulation tape, which I use on the spots where the seals have started to leak.

"This is just a temporary solution," I say.

As I'm cleaning the pipes, she tells me that she had just graduated as a librarian when the war broke out and she worked in the children's department of a library.

"We tried to live a normal life in between our escapes. I took on whatever jobs came my way and in the meantime Fifi took care of Adam. Sometimes I was paid, sometimes not."

Once the water acquires a natural colour and pressure, she brings me the bedside lamp and shows me the wiring. She says she changed the bulb, but the lamp doesn't work so she was wondering if it might be something else.

I immediately see the plug needs to be changed.

She nods with a grave and apprehensive air.

"It can be complicated to get spare parts," she explains, adjusting a lock of hair. "The stores are out of stock. You have to have connections," she adds.

The words of the man in the leopard socks in the hall echo in my mind: you can buy anything if you have the right contacts.

Then she's suddenly positioned herself in front of me with her hands planted on her hips and wants more detailed information on my real purpose here.

"It's not at all convincing that you are here on vacation," she says. "With a drill."

She tugs the elastic out of her hair and then almost immediately slips it back on again.

I remain silent. I'm good at remaining silent.

"Mom said you didn't talk," Waterlily said. That isn't quite true, however, since at the beginning of our relationship, I did. *I spoke and G was silent,* it says in the diary entry about our hike in the mountains.

She looks me in the eye and won't give up.

"Why are you here?"

I hesitate and stop myself from repeating that I'm on vacation. Instead I say:

"I'm not sure."

She scrutinises me.

"Have you come to collect something? Buy something?"

"No."

"Sell something?"

"No. I have no plans."

I can't tell this young woman, who has been through so much to survive with her son and younger brother under showers of bombs—in a country in which blood flows through the river beds where firing squads passed a few weeks ago, dying the water red—that I have come all this way to kill myself. I can't explain to these people that I've come here with my toolbox to set up a hook, that I travel with my drill the way others travel with their toothbrush. I can't tell her—after all she's been through—that I'm going to saddle her and her brother with the chore of taking me down. My unhappiness is at best inane when compared to the ruins and dust that lie outside my window.

Do you know? It's spring tears,
spring tears that fall on the black sand

When I'm alone again I open up the door onto the balcony.
It takes some time to wrestle with it because the hotel hasn't
been heated for a long time and the wood has swollen. It
would have been best if I had a hand plane to smooth the
edge, but I manage to solve the problem with a few sheets
of sandpaper I brought with me. While I'm at it, I tighten
two screws on the handles. On the balcony there are pots
of withered flowers, so I fill the toothbrush glass with water
and pour it over the plants. I do it in a total of four trips.

The sea is closer than I'd expected and gives off a scent
of very ripe, sweet fruit. I don't have to look long to realise
that this is totally different than the churning ocean I'm
used to, there are no giant waves here, as heavy as slamming metal doors, no swirling white mounds of surf that
pull up stones and suck down boats; what appears before
me from my window is a giant, salty swimming pool or a
floating mirror.

I pay no heed to the recommendation to stay along the
path to the deserted shore, but on my way I notice that the
firewood shed is almost empty.

"No one's willing to chop firewood," the girl had said.

Should I walk into the sea?

How far out does one have to swim to exhaust one's self?

A bird swirls above me.

One circle.

Will he dive down and strike me?

Two circles.

He lands. I notice the bird is limping and finding it difficult to take off again. In a country of warfare and dust even the animals are maimed; dogs hop on three paws, cats have one eye, birds one leg.

As I'm standing on the beach I suddenly remember the pod of whales Gudrún and I once drove past on the coast, where five or six of them had swum ashore and become stranded. We grabbed shovels from the boot and dug holes at the water's edge to try to keep them alive and get them floating again.

"It's important," she said when we got back to the car, "to share memories."

Had we stopped sleeping together by then?

I remove my socks and shoes, stand in the cold mud until a salty puddle forms around me and sucks me down. When the foam reaches my ankles I turn away.

If it is possible to compare the two, me and the world

When I get back I turn on the shower, take off my clothes— the same I arrived in—and stand naked on the cold floor. The water isn't red anymore now that I've fixed the pipes.

Before me is a mirror and in it the outline of an unknown male body with a snow-white water lily on his chest, over the heart. Like a stamped trademark on a pale sailcloth. I haven't examined myself in a mirror for many years, not all of me. Have I ever done that? The mirrors back in my apartment hadn't been designed for a man who was one metre eighty-five centimetres tall. I used the mirror in the bathroom to shave, not look at myself.

I've got skinny, Mom would say.

I'm exposed. Ludicrous.

I feel the muscles in my upper arms and my stomach, but find it difficult to discern *whether I'm the person in the mirror or the other.*

I still have all my hair, as Mom rightly points out. Like the bristles of a brush pointing in the air. And the hair barely white.

On one side there is me and, on the other, my body. Both equally strangers.

Were we together in school, did I meet that guy the summer I worked on tarring the roads, were we acquaintances? Is this the young man who pondered celestial bodies?

The sun hasn't shone on this body for some time. Not as a whole. I haven't sunbathed for seventeen years. It was an unusually hot June day, seventeen degrees in the shade, so I allowed myself to be in swimming trunks as I was nailing boxes around ten strawberry plants for Gudrún. I didn't lie down because I'm a *Homo erectus*, an upright man who is always busy doing something.

Gudrún lay sunbathing beside the strawberry beds in the ocean breeze, ginger-haired with a pinkish-red complexion, bit by bit the freckles merged. Every now and then, she hoisted herself on her elbows to spread some tanning lotion on some part of her body. She had a book, read a few lines, and then closed her eyes in between. There was a bush nearby and, after a short while, a shadow formed and she got up with the rug and moved to a patch of the lawn with less shade.

I turn on the light in the new bedroom. All the lamps are working. Soon darkness stretches over the town like a woollen blanket and it gets cooler. A dog howls—is it the one with three legs?—and then vanishes.

What shall I do until I sleep?

I fetch one of the diaries and sit on the bed. It's the middle one. The two of us are here together, my former self and my present self, the boy and the middle-aged man.

What makes a boy write: *Thanks for life, Mom.* Why not Dad? I thank Mom for giving birth to me and girls for sleeping with me. I'm a man who expresses gratitude.

Mom says she had wished she'd had a daughter.

I too would certainly have liked a sister. Instead I had girlfriends. That I slept with. Four in the same week, if the diary entries are anything to go by.

Apart from that, I have a very foggy image of that boy who describes cloud formations and female bodies. It's clearly something we have in common, he and I, that he doesn't know who he is any more than I do.

I don't exist yet is written in clear letters under the date 24 October.

A few pages later there is a sentence I have crossed out with one fine stroke of the pen, but that is still legible: ~~How did I become me?~~

N regularly appears in entries beside the other letters—K, A, L, S, and G—but I don't have to read far to realise that it isn't a girl I've slept with, because in one place N is fully named as Friedrich Nietzsche. On the basis of the dates and quotations here and there, I spent a whole year reading *Beyond Good and Evil*. That was my year at university. My diary seems to have served as a glossary.

Whatever remains in him of "person" seems accidental, often arbitrary, and disruptive. It takes effort to think on "himself," he's not infrequently mistaken when he does. He confuses himself with others, he is wrong about his basic needs.

My attention is drawn to the fact that death is omnipresent, appearing at three-page intervals along with that *wonderful experience of suffering.*

Two days after Dad's death, I write: *People die. Other people. One dies. By "one" I mean myself. I die. Because life is the most delicate thing of all. If I have children they'll die as well. When it comes to that, I won't be with my children to hold their hands, to comfort them.*

And an entry on the following fourteenth of April reads:

125

At our latitudes people mostly kill themselves in the spring. People can't bear the idea of the earth renewing itself. Of everything starting anew except themselves.

This isn't a bad boy. He's innocent and well-meaning. I notice how weather and cloud descriptions are gradually supplanted by environmental concerns, with entries about the thinning of the ozone layer, greenhouse gases, and global warming. *The glaciers recede and eventually disappear. In just a few decades these vast water reservoirs of the world will have disappeared.*

What would I say to that boy today? If he was my son, I mean?

I turn the page.

The following is written at the top of the next:

I don't believe in God anymore and I fear he no longer believes in me.

I swiftly skim through the diary.

On the second-to-last page it transpires that my former self gave blood.

Went to the blood bank and donated blood. And below—on a new line—three words: *I feel dizzy.*

As far as I can make out, the visit to the blood bank gave rise to two pretty interesting reports on the final page.

Places where I've done it:

Bed (A, K, L, D, G, S), graveyard (E), car (K), staircase (H), bathroom (L), summer house (K), public swimming pool (S), crater (with G).

And straight after that:

List of places I haven't done it: blood bank, art museum, police station (etc.).

I close the diary and turn off the light. What thought should I choose while I lull myself into the darkness? I'm sitting with Gudrún Waterlily in my arms on a carousel—she chose a unicorn—and her mother, my wife, waves at us—while everything spins and the world expands at the speed of light. We wave back at her. Then the world slows down again and shrinks into a tiny iris, just before it's switched off, before I'm switched off.

The wonderful experience, the suffering, ignites hope

I have no change of clothes, apart from the single shirt dangling on a wooden hanger in the wardrobe. What am I to do about that? Why didn't I take any clothes with me? I get my red shirt and put it on.

I rub my jaw. Shouldn't I shave? I haven't shaved in four days.

"The hotel shop might have razors," said May.

I ring the bell and wait for Fifi to appear.

"Did May mention we had razors?" he says when I ask him.

He has stepped behind the reception desk in a hoodie and jeans. He's not wearing his white shirt, but I notice he

127

has white dust in his hair, as if he'd sprinkled flour over it. He's taken the headphones off his ears.

"Yes, she mentioned a hotel shop."

"That was packed away in the war. That was actually before my time," he adds after some thought.

He opens a drawer, rummages through it, and finally fishes out a bundle of keys.

"I think this is the one for the storage room," he says, beckoning me to follow him down a corridor behind the reception desk, then down a staircase to a locked door.

It takes him some time to find the right key.

"There should be a storage room here," he explains as he tries out the keys.

The young man seems to be just as dumbfounded as I am when he opens the door and gropes at length for a light switch.

The room is quite large, windowless and crammed with an assortment of items, souvenirs and all kinds of gifts that have been stacked on rows of shelves, but also in boxes on the floor. In the middle, there is a postcard stand and another one with sunglasses. On the shelves there are swimsuits with price tags, goggles, toys, inflatables, and towels. I'm transfixed by inflated brightly coloured animals that have shrivelled and lost their shape: a green crocodile with a limp jaw, a totally deflated leopard, a yellow giraffe, a purple dolphin. I also spot a box full of ballpoint pens with "Hotel Silence" inscribed on them.

This is undoubtedly the hotel storage room. The remains of a world that was. The remains of a world of bright colours.

Fifi moves some objects, shuffling them from hand to hand, like a child in a toy shop, and is visibly bewildered.

"I haven't explored everything at the hotel," he explains. "May and I have only been here five months."

It is clear from his expression that he doesn't know where to start.

"They should be somewhere, razors."

And he sidesteps between the piles on the floor, opening boxes and cartons containing suntan lotions, lip balms, soaps, colouring books, postcards, and sealed hotel tooth-brushes.

In one corner of the room is a half-open box that turns out to be full of books.

"I think these are books that the hotel guests left behind," says the young man after a brief examination.

He digs into the box.

"They're in different languages," he concludes.

I bend over and run my fingers over the volumes: there's Thomas Mann, *The Magic Mountain* and also *Doctor Faustus*; *Jerusalem* by Selma Lagerlöf; a collection of poems by Emily Dickinson; *Leaves of Grass* by Walt Whitman; *A Room of One's Own* by Virginia Woolf; and another poetry book by Elizabeth Bishop. I open it, skim through and read some lines about how *The art of losing isn't hard to master*. Because *so many things seem filled with the intent / to be lost,* Bishop writes, the author who herself had lost a watch, mother, house, cities, two rivers and a continent.

Lose something every day. Accept the fluster
of lost door keys . . .

I put the poetry book back into the box and pick up Yeats, browse through a few pages and pause on: *Things fall apart, the centre cannot hold.*

The young man observes me inspecting the books.

"Someone must have wanted to get rid of those books because they didn't like them enough to keep them. You're welcome to take some, if you like. May told me you're a writer yourself."

He stoops over the boxes and seems to be puzzled by everything they contain.

"I wanted to study history," he says, "that's if I'd gone to college. But ever since I realised that it's only written by the victors, I don't want to anymore."

He straightens up and is holding a packet of disposable plastic razors.

"We only have Venus, pink," he says, handing me the bag. Six of them.

I'll try them. I tell the young man I'll also take a ballpoint pen out of the box and shove it into my breast pocket.

He asks me if I need anything else.

"No, I don't think so."

"Condoms, mister Jónas?"

"No, thanks."

He says he's not too sure about how to price the goods, but that he'll stick the razors on my bill.

I notice him scanning the room and moving things on the shelves as if he were searching for something.

I decide to make use of the intimacy of this space to mention the mosaic mural one more time. When I'd bumped into him the last time, he had said that the remarkable thing about this wall I was asking about was that there was absolutely no trace of it, and no one was aware of hot springs in the area.

"It's all very strange," he had said.

This time he hesitates and I seize on the opportunity to insist some more. Yes, that's right, he now remembers that there are some hot springs in the area and he confirms that there are, in fact, baths in the basement of the hotel, but that they are closed at the moment.

The answer regarding the mosaic mural is noncommittal, however.

"That's right, there were"—he uses the past tense—"somewhere around here some famous murals, but they're not accessible to tourists right now."

He continues to open boxes while he's talking, looking into them and closing them again.

"Will they be soon?"

He hesitates again.

"Well, they're actually packed away."

131

He's standing by the postcard stand and gives it a spin.

"Since we're starting to get tourists again, maybe we should try putting a few of these in the lobby," he says.

Yearning is stronger than pain

There are three of us sitting at as many tables for breakfast. I see that the actress is by the window with her slice of bread and cup of coffee. There is a pile of papers on her table. I have greeted her three times. The neighbour from my corridor sits at the third table, and that's the sum of the guests. The coloured paper lanterns that hang from the ceiling draw my attention because the room seems to have been decorated for a feast.

"From the beginning of the war," says Fifi, when he brings the coffee over. The wedding was cancelled in the end. They used to hold a ball here too once a year. For New Year's.

Honey is offered for the bread and I remember what I read online about bee breeding when I was booking the hotel. Fifi also told me that the bees died during the war and honey production has ceased.

When the actress sees me, she smiles and stands up, takes her coffee cup, gathers her pile of papers, and walks towards me. I notice that my neighbour from the corridor is watching both of us, and adjusting his chair and posture to keep us clearly in sight. He is wearing a yellow velvet jacket, Bermuda shorts, and striped socks.

Alfred, he said his name was.

The actress asks if she can sit with me, puts down her papers, and adjusts a scarf around her neck.

Slowly.

Then she says she saw me down on the beach.

"Yes, I was checking to see if the sea was salty."

She smiles.

"And was it?"

"Yes, it was."

She gazes out the window.

"That isn't the same sea you have in your parts."

"No, it's not the same sea we have in our parts."

A woman speaks to me and I've immediately started to repeat her. She says she was born and raised in this country but moved abroad long before the war.

"We shot a movie here back then. It was popular to shoot films in these parts that were meant to be set somewhere else completely."

She speaks, I shut up.

I like to sit opposite a woman and to shut up.

"I stood here on the last day of the shoot," she says, pointing at the square in front of the hotel. "My costar stood there," she continues, pointing again. "He stretched out his hand when a shot was fired. The filming went badly. We did the scene six times and used gallons of artificial blood. We had good fun in the evening. It was all make-believe. Then it turned into reality and the movie felt phoney."

She suddenly falls silent and looks around. The man from room number nine has disappeared.

"In the months preceding the outbreak of hostilities, people started to vanish from the face of the earth, journalists, university lecturers, artists. Then ordinary people from next door. People weren't prepared for the need to adopt the right opinions about the government. Entire families disappeared like they'd never existed. By then the country was suddenly full of weapons."

We both shut up.

"People are gripped by despair when they realise what the situation is, but can't change it," she says finally.

She leans over the table and looks straight at me. And lowers her voice.

"There used to be a zoo in town," she continues, "but the animals were shot at the beginning of the war. They say that one wild animal managed to escape. People aren't sure of the species, but they say it was a big male beast, some say a tiger, others a leopard, and others again a panther. Various stories are told about what became of it. Some even say the beast is managing the reconstruction."

She adjusts the scarf around her neck again, finishes her cup of coffee, and scoops the sugar from the bottom with a spoon.

Then she says she's on her way into the country but will be back in ten days. Her plan is to visit some members of her family, but also to scout for locations for a documentary and look for interviewees.

"The documentary is about how women handle communities after a war," she adds, brandishing a rolled-up script. "They also shoulder the responsibility for keeping the family together and it's a terrible strain."

She says something else, but I'm thinking of the emphasis she placed on the fact that she is returning. She wants to know if I will have left when she comes back.

"Will you be gone? In ten days' time?" she asks with feigned nonchalance.

I reflect on this. In the land of death there isn't the same urgency to die.

"No, I don't expect to be gone," I say. And I think, this is the kind of place to linger in.

There are so many voices in the world and
none of them is without meaning

May is waiting for me when I return to the room. She has a formal request to make. That's precisely how she words it:

"I have a formal request for you," she says.

She's wearing a black blouse and draws a deep breath as she shuffles her feet in the doorway.

135

"My brother and I had a chat and decided to ask you if you could help us with some small repairs at the hotel. To be more precise, a few small jobs."

She pauses.

"That is to say, when you're not sightseeing." The use of the term sightseeing seems slightly alien to her.

She says they can't pay me much for it because they haven't had many tourists yet, that is to say, apart from the three of us—me, the lady, and the man—and therefore they've had no revenue yet. They would rather pay with bed and board. It occurred to her, for example, that I might want to prolong my stay and extend my vacation with more vacation. She says this hesitantly, as if she were trying out the words together, vacation and vacation. And stay for an extra two weeks. Even three. That would include room and breakfast.

"Fifi and I discussed this last night and we agree."

What exactly they agree on, she doesn't say.

She edges into the room and stands in front of me. Her hair is in a ponytail, like Waterlily's.

"There's a shortage of men," she says. "And tools. Those who didn't die in the war or flee the country are busy doing other things. A whole generation of men disappeared. Foreign contractors don't fix cupboard doors and doorknobs."

I tell her what I've told her before, that I'm neither a carpenter nor a plumber. And not an electrician either.

"You have a drill."

I give this some thought.

Since I've already told the actress that I will be here when she comes back in about a week's time, I need to have something to do. Which is why I say:

"I really want to help you. I can't do everything," I add, "but I can do some things."

She smiles from ear to ear.

Then she turns serious again.

"Any chance you could start tomorrow?"

"If you like, I can start straightaway," I say.

HOMO HABILIS I
(HANDYMAN I)

There are sixteen bedrooms and it takes us a while to find the keys that fit the locks. We move between floors and May opens and closes doors. We step into dusty rooms, she pulls back the curtains and shows me what needs to be fixed.

Most of them are small repairs I can easily cope with, although I would have wanted to have better tools with me. I think of my bigger toolboxes in my basement on the other side of the ocean. It transpires that many of the cupboard doors are hanging on just one hinge, and locks, knobs, and window handles need to be repaired. I also need to check the pipes, switches, wiring, plugs, and sockets.

Each room has its own design but all have a fireplace, with a gilt-framed mirror over the mantle, and a forest landscape painting over the bed featuring an animal and a hunter. Their other common feature is the fact that they haven't been heated for a long time so the same musty smell hovers in the air. There are fissures and damp patches in a number of places on the walls and cracking paint on the ceiling. The leafy wallpaper which is to be found on one or two walls of each room is worn-out and has started to peel at the seams.

I don't mention paint to the girl, since I assume it is difficult to come by. The furniture, on the other hand, is of good quality and, on the whole, the hotel is in a pretty good state.

"Compared to the rest of the country," as May emphasises.

I explain that, to begin with, the rooms need to be aired to get the dampness out of the walls. All of the floors have threadbare handwoven rugs and I suggest we roll them up and carry them outside to beat the dust out of them.

As we're rolling up the first rug, beautiful turquoise tiles are revealed with peculiar square patterns reminiscent of a maze.

We stand in the middle of the floor admiring the tiling.

"Yes, I think this was the old town centre," she says, and explains how each town has—or had—its own particular pattern, its tiling. Turquoise is the signature colour of this town and is to be found in the old neighbouring mines. This matches the information I found about the mosaic mural that no one seems to have heard of or can trace.

She circles the room looking at the tiles and I hear her say that her father was a palaeographer and some of his friends were archaeologists. I omit to tell her I drove past the ruins of the National Archive on the way to the hotel. She has nothing else to say about the tiles, but instead sinks onto the bed, bowing her head. Her palms turned upwards.

"My father was the head of the manuscript department of the National Archive and he was shot at work. We were allowed to collect his body from the street corner where it was abandoned."

She falls silent.

"You can't show a child his grandfather who has been shot in the head," she adds.

I lift up the rolled carpet, lean it vertically against some corner of the room, drag over a chair and sit opposite her.

"Mom waited too long to flee," she says in a low voice.

Could I tell this young woman in a skirt and blue blouse with two unfastened top buttons that sometimes *men shall beat their swords into ploughshares*? Would that sound meaningless? To say that it's possible to be human again after being a wild beast? Or is it impossible maybe?

She pulls a handkerchief out of her pocket and blows her nose.

"Suddenly the country was crammed with weapons and one day the war was here in a flash. All kinds of stories were being told and no one could work out what was going on."

She pauses then continues.

"We didn't know who we were supposed to believe because everyone said the same thing, that they had been attacked by the evil forces out of the blue. Everyone said that the enemy had killed women and innocent children and showed photos of the victims. Everyone said there was no choice but to defend themselves."

She shook her head.

"I don't know how so much hatred spread across the community. All of a sudden everyone hated everyone."

This makes me think of Mom. "At the core of evil, there's a desire for revenge," she used to say. "Hatred breeds hatred, and bloodshed leads to more bloodshed," she'd add.

"It was no problem to die," May finally says, looking me in the eye with quivering lips. "I wasn't afraid of being shot or blown to pieces, but if they captured you, then you'd die a hundred times."

HOMO HABILIS 2
(HANDYMAN 2)

She walks ahead and I follow with my toolbox.

"Fix," she says, and I fix.

I unscrew the showerheads, and in many cases it seems to be sufficient to clear the sand and pebbles out of the pipes for the water to regain its natural pressure and colour. Then I do the same for the sinks. I suggest we get rid of the threadbare rugs and allow the tiles to shine in all their glory.

"You're so tall you don't need a chair to change a light bulb," she says, as I'm standing on a chair to change a light bulb in the ceiling, and I swiftly glance at my reflection in the mirror over the fireplace. I don't tell her that less than a week ago I stood on a chair, groping for a fixture, for a hook. The chair is wobbly and I waver as if I were on a tightrope. I'm in my red shirt and underneath it is the white water lily and underneath the water lily lies a bloody heart that is still beating. I stretch out my arms, pumping up my red chest like a bird that is about to take flight. Then I jump off the chair and reach into the bag of light bulbs.

As we're working, she talks to me.

As she's talking, I work.

Sometimes she abruptly stops what she is doing and says things like:

"We had a piano."

Or she says:

"Once I found a finger on the street. It had a wedding ring on it. What was I supposed to do with a finger?"

Or:

"When I woke up, it took me one to two minutes to remember there was a war. Those were the best minutes

141

in the day." I calculate in my mind; Mom would have immediately answered that there are 1,440 minutes in a day.

"And if there was silence, you knew that it would all start again tomorrow."

She also sometimes says something that makes me think: She's like me. I used to think like that as well. Or she says something and I know she is thinking about something else. Or she is on the point of saying something but then stops and shuts up.

The boy follows his usual routine, crawling around his mother and vanishing at intervals. He is timid and holds himself at a safe distance from me, and I sense his wariness. I also sense a growing curiosity in him, which gradually subdues his fears. I notice he has a keen interest in the toolbox and eventually he steps in to hand me a screw. It's difficult to establish any eye contact with him and if I show any interest or try to talk to him, he runs away. When he draws nearer I see he has a large scar over his eyebrow.

"A rat," says his mother. "He was bitten by a rat when we were sleeping on a mouldy floor in a basement for a few months, on the run."

As soon as I pick up the drill, the boy covers his ears and scurries under the table. There he sits with his chin pressed against his knees, blocking both ears.

"He thinks that's a gun," says his mother.

A few moments later, he is up again and has dragged a chair into the centre of the room and sits on it, at a comfortable distance, to watch us work. I hear him talking to himself.

"He's started talking again," May says. "He didn't speak for a whole year."

The boy isn't happy not to understand what we are saying. His mother says something to him and I get the feeling she is giving him a summary of our conversation because he is nodding and looking at us, alternately.

I notice that when she talks to him he tilts his head and turns his left ear to her. She confirms my suspicion that the boy has damaged hearing.

"Almost everyone who lived through the air raids lost some or all of their hearing. At first it was the sound of gunfire in the neighbourhood, then the exploding bombs."

She seems to have grown pensive, there is a distant look in her eyes.

"At first there was a whistle, then a yellow flash in the sky, then a shock wave like something slamming against the walls. Even if it was night it was blindingly bright for one moment. There was a constant pounding in our ears and all our muscles tensed up for days, weeks, and months on end."

Svanur comes to mind.

"In any case, it's clear that a man dies alone," he had said as we were standing on the pier under the sinking red sun. "Unless one lives in a country of air raids. Then there's a good chance of an entire family being wiped out at the exact same moment."

What appears before the eyes

I wonder if something else could be found for the boy to do other than run about with a towel-cape around his shoulders looking for hiding places. I mention it to May.

"He finds it difficult to sit still," she says.

It occurs to me that he could draw, I seem to remember spotting a drawing pad and a box of coloured pencils in the hotel shop.

While I'm waiting for Fifi to show up, I notice that the postcard stand has been reinstalled in the reception area. I give the stand a twirl and glance at the cards: a carefree couple sits on a bench in a flower-adorned square eating ice cream, young women sunbathe on the beach while muscular thighs play in the breaking waves. What strikes me are the bright colours, the vibrant blue sky and golden sand; the world was still in colour back then and people didn't know what was in store, they're alive, both their legs are still of the same length, they have plans for the future, maybe they're going to change cars or kitchen units or take a trip abroad. Above all, though, my attention is drawn to the postcards that show a large mosaic mural from different angles, several with details of it or as a whole. The subject matter is naked women wrapped in thin transparent veils; one woman is fetching water from a stream, another is bathing, and another again is stooping over the closed petals of a flower. I turn one of the cards over, it says on the back in three languages that the work is to be found at Hotel Silence. It all fits with the information I read online.

I brandish the card when the young man appears.

"This is the mosaic I was asking about." He bends over and seems to be carefully examining the card, clutching its corner between his index finger and his thumb, and I realise that he's pondering something, to gain time.

"Yes, May and I have been wanting to talk to you about the mosaic wall," he finally says.

He chooses his words carefully and speaks slowly.

"The thing is, at first, May and I thought you'd come here for the artwork. And that that was why you had a toolbox with you."

He hesitates.

"You see, ancient artefacts have actually been disappearing from the country." And he explains to me that he has been instructed not to talk about antiquities to foreigners.

"We had to be sure you weren't on the same kind of mission as the other guest."

"The other guest" is presumably the man in the room next to me. "After a war everything is up for grabs," he'd said.

"I told May you'd bought a razor. And taken a ballpoint pen. And that you'd come back three times to return a book and take another out of the box."

He turns the stand to put the postcard in its place.

"But now that you've virtually become a staff member at the hotel, the situation has completely changed," he adds, lowering his voice. "My sister and I have decided that you can take a look at the mosaic mural, if you like. Whenever it suits you."

THREE BREASTS

I follow Fifi down to the basement, past the storage room, and through a door which he opens and closes with a key.

The mural that appears before us is huge, bigger than I expected, and divided into two. On one side is the original wall, the antiquity the town prides itself on, and which was discovered when it was dug up during the construction of the hotel. On the other side, there is a kind of continuation of the wall, with more recent tiling that was probably added when the hotel was built. The original wall is separated from the baths by a glass wall, but the hotel's spa baths are dry, no water.

"The baths were first built six hundred years ago," the young man explains.

We stand side by side, two men, taking in this manless world, masses of flesh flash before us, chubby female forms, small breasts like half-lemons, thin waists, broad hips. How many bodies did I get to know before I met Gudrún? K makes two appearances in the diary, there was B and M and twice E, is it the same E? Then there's J and P and S, who appear three times. If I compare these bodies to those of the women I have known intimately—I dig deep—I come to the conclusion that I don't remember them as a whole; I remember segments of bodies, one breast, I might remember a wrist, I remember a white neck, skin texture, or whether a lamp was on, maybe there was an open wardrobe door through which I could see a dress on a hanger—but I don't remember a complete body.

In the background one can see the same turquoise colour as the tiles in the bedroom, not unlike the hue of the icebergs on the Jökulsárlón lagoon back home by the pitch-black sand.

"The stones catch the light," Fifi explains. "That's why it looks like the light is glowing from inside the wall."

What interests me the most, though, is the fact that some sections of the mural seem to have been cut out of the wall here and there and lie in scattered pieces around the floor.

He explains that antiquities and relics of cultural value were systematically destroyed in the war, which was why they had been hidden or moved. The plan had been to transfer the mural to save it, which is why they had started to rip down parts of it.

In one spot a woman is missing a breast, in another an arm, a crotch in another, a missing heel, a missing wrist, a missing ear, and missing buttocks.

"I've been trying to sort through the fragments and to work out what goes where and mark them. I think I've found all the pieces except for three breasts. They should be here somewhere," he says, looking around.

I notice he has placed handwritten labels on some of the fragments.

"People don't know how to work properly," he says apologetically, adding that they're expecting a group of archaeologists to evaluate the damage to the wall. Within a few weeks. Hopefully.

The new wall is altogether different and, as far as I can make out, seems to have been made with ordinary bathroom tiles. The subject matter is the same—naked female bodies—but the execution and anatomy are completely different; big breasts, small childlike hips, and long skinny legs like insects.

"Barbie," Fifi comments with a smile, and I nod.

It's the tile fragments the young man has been working on. There is a bowl of plaster on the floor and beside it a trowel and other tools. Ceramic fragments lie in bundles on the floor.

"I'm trying to fix it," he says, pointing at the cracks where the tiling has crumbled. "We're planning to get the baths working again by next year. If the truce holds."

He doesn't seem to have a lot of confidence in his repairs and it's obvious that he doesn't know how to handle a trowel. I've tiled enough bathrooms to wonder whether he is using the right joint filling.

I knock on the wall, the cracks don't seem to be deep. But more of the tiling needs to come off and the underlying layer needs to be cleaned before new ones go up.

"I consulted a curator and he said that the repairs should be visible," he says hesitantly. "He was a friend of Dad's."

He suddenly falls silent and turns away.

His hands are shaking.

Then he picks up the thread again.

"Otherwise it's in pretty good condition, compared to other things in this country."

His sister had said the same thing.

FIFI

On the way back upstairs, I stop by the storage room to look for a drawing pad. Fifi says he has started to sort through the stuff and has obviously shifted some boxes around, as well as moving the postcard stand to the lobby. But it's impossible to make out what exactly has been sorted. We help each other move some things and I find a drawing pad and also dig up some coloured pencils and markers.

He says he's found another box full of unclaimed property and points at an open one on the floor.

"It's incredible what some people take on their holidays and don't miss when they leave." He gropes through the box.

"Here's a wedding certificate, silver sugar tongs, a passport, a real estate contract, a wedding ring—just one—inscribed with the initials LL."

He hands me the ring to examine and says he searched for the matching one, but hasn't found it.

"So they weren't together when they removed them," he adds.

Then he remembers something he has been meaning to mention to me.

"There might be some tools in the basement. What did you say you needed?"

I list off several tools and tell him what they're used for. I end by mentioning a carpenter's plane.

He wrinkles his forehead as if trying to solve a riddle.

"No, I don't think there's anything that fits that description," he answers. "Maybe it would be best if you just take a look yourself," he adds.

I look around.

Could that be a bag of light bulbs glinting on the top shelf under the ceiling? Yes, it looks like it. Then we don't have to keep swapping light bulbs from the lamps in the rooms that aren't being used. Behind the light bulbs there is an elongated object enveloped in Bubble Wrap. I take it down and hand it to the young man. The parcel is quite heavy and looks fragile. He cautiously places it on the floor and we stare at it a moment before he starts to pull off the tape and unwrap it. We've both fallen silent. Once he's removed the plastic, the vase emerges. It's made of ice-blue glass, with a gilded overlay of patterns not unlike those to be found on the bedroom floors, but in a more minute form. I realise it must be a genuine antique.

"So there it is," says the young man. "We've been looking for this. It disappeared from the municipal museum. We thought it had been sold abroad."

He carefully wraps the vase back up in plastic and holds it in his arms like a newborn child.

Then he nods at the goods I've collected.

"It's difficult to price that," he says. He hesitates.

"I'll put it on your bill."

He immediately corrects himself.

"I'll deduct it from your wages."

A darkness was upon the face of the deep

I place the drawing pad and coloured pencils on the desk of the bedroom we are working on, but Adam shows no interest in them. He doesn't want to draw and prefers to handle the tools. He shoots past me and positions himself in front of the toolbox. He wants to be allowed to hold the screwdriver. He is waiting for us men to start our daily work.

"Mister Jónas."

He's learned my name.

His mother beckons him back to the desk, puts a cushion under him on the chair, places a sheet from the drawing pad in front of him, and asks him something. I'm guessing she's asking what colour he wants to use because she opens the box of pencils and hands him a blue one. He immediately throws it on the floor. She hands him another colour and he throws that one on the floor as well, and pushes away the box of pencils.

He's angry.

He's not going to draw a sun and bright sky today. Or a rainbow.

His mom lets him sulk, but a short while later has to pop out and calls the boy.

He shakes his head.

She explains something to him, I sense she's trying to persuade him, but he doesn't move.

"He wants to stay with you," she says.

"That's okay," I answer. "I could be his granddad," I add, but immediately realise that requires further explanation.

"My daughter is the same age as you," I say.

"He can't talk to you," she says hesitantly.

"Then we'll both be quiet."

"You're so closed in," Gudrún would have said.

"I won't be long, an hour at the most."

"No problem," I repeat.

The second his mom closes the door behind her, the boy leaps off the chair to fetch the screwdriver.

"Later," I say.

I sit at the desk and make him understand I'm about to make a drawing.

He observes me from a distance and I see that he's not satisfied.

What am I going to draw?

I reach for the purple pencil and draw a box. Then I change colours and draw a red triangle on top of the box. It's a house with a roof. Then he suddenly darts over to the table, snatches the sheet of paper, tears it in two and tramples on it. He hands me a black pencil. I'm not allowed to use colours.

"All right," I say, "we'll just use black today."

I take a new sheet and draw another house. Then I draw a chair inside it. The boy looks at me questioningly. I add another chair, then more furniture.

He slowly edges closer and finally stands silently right behind me, looking over my shoulder.

When the house is finished, I draw people inside; a man and a woman and two children, a girl and a boy. He has suddenly crawled under the bed. I see his laced plimsolls under the mattress but leave him in peace.

I liked to be left in peace when I was his age. When he reemerges from under the bed I fetch a glass of water and hand it to him. He drinks the water and then heads straight for the desk, eases himself onto the chair, grabs the black pencil and draws a streak across the sheet. Then another streak and a third streak until the page is full of black strokes

153

and a black cluster has formed in the middle. I watch him. Once he has filled the sheet with darkness, he rips the drawing to shreds and throws it on the floor. I place another sheet in front of him. He looks at the box of colours and hesitates a moment before he reaches for the red and attacks the sheet. He doesn't look up until he's finished the work. This drawing is like the previous one, except it's red. The world is a blazing fire.

I nod.

He pushes the box of colours away, his day's work is done, and he positions himself by the toolbox. He wants to turn to real work. Show me what he's made of.

LIMBO

In the evening I go back to Restaurant Limbo. Normally it's the same dish two days in a row, but now the owner has added a new one and offers me a choice.

"We've expanded the menu," he says, and asks if I'd like soup with dumplings or stew like yesterday. I go for the soup.

I've noticed that he, like other people in the town, frequently talks in the first person plural. But I have yet to spot another staff member or customer in this place.

The soup with little dumplings floating in it arrives after a brief wait.

The owner behaves as he did last time, standing by the table as I eat with a tea cloth draped over his shoulder. Then the monologue begins. He starts off by telling me what I've been doing and says he's heard that I've chatted with the actress and that I've been seen on the football pitch and that he's also heard I didn't follow the path to the beach.

The next thing he says is that he sees I've shaved. He also hasn't failed to notice that I'm wearing the same red shirt and to draw the conclusion that I need a change of clothes. He says he can pull a few strings and talk to the owner of a shop down the street.

"The problem is that it's closed, but not really closed," he says.

The owner has a small stockroom, but one has to phone him to place an order. How many shirts do I need and what else apart from shirts? A belt?

If, on the other hand, I need a suit, he knows a guy who knows a guy who knows another guy who can tailor a suit for me out of the best material. He himself has a tailor-made jacket. He's in his shirt, but his jacket is on a hanger in the cloakroom by the entrance. He fetches the jacket and puts it on. As he's about to show me the lining, a revolver flashes in the inside pocket. He swiftly removes the jacket again and hangs it on a hook.

"It would be nice to wake up without having killed anyone," he says as he adjusts the jacket.

After a moment's thought, he adds:

"You just don't know if the truce will last."

I notice a photograph of a young married couple hanging on the wall. It occurs to me that the reception must have been held here. I have no recollection of photographs being taken at my and Gudrún's wedding. We got married in a cold spring rain and she wore a light blue dress. It was open in the back and I thought that was beautiful.

I ask him about the photograph:

"My daughter," he says, turning away to dab the corners of his eyes with the tea cloth.

Then the report continues. In addition to wandering alone on the beach, he says he has heard I've taken on additional odd jobs for the siblings at Hotel Silence.

I give nothing away about that.

"We heard that you have black tape," he said, "and can fix anything."

Judging by his expression, he'd like me to confirm this. He says that he's heard I fix lamps.

"So you do electrical things as well, not only plumbing."

"It's temporary," I say.

After the soup he wants me to have coffee and pulls up a chair to sit opposite me at the table. He wants me to work for him and brings up the swinging doors he had mentioned the other day.

"Wing doors," he reiterates.

It transpires that he has been working on a new drawing, a new version of the doors.

"With measurements," he says.

He pulls a sheet out of his breast pocket, carefully unfolds it, brushes the crumbs off the table with his hand, and places the drawing in front of me. I notice that he has drawn in shadowing and scribbled numbers.

He says he's improved the quality of the drawing, as he puts it.

I ask if he's managed to procure the tools. He says he's working on it.

"What tools were they again?" he asks gingerly. It's obvious from his expression that he hasn't fully grasped the concept of this project, so I turn the sheet around and indicate that I want to draw. He doesn't want me to ruin his original work, so he gets me a new sheet and I sketch out various tools with the ballpoint pen marked "Hotel Silence."

He nods.

Then he wants to draw.

It takes some time, during which I glance around. No sign of the cat.

He pushes the paper over to me. He seems to have drawn a pipe wrench and a roll of sealing tape.

And he adds:

"There is a leaking sink."

The next time I come he says he's going to offer me meat in a sauce with prunes.

"Old recipe. Speciality. From my grandmother."

157

He dabs the corners of his eyes with the teacloth again. Before I leave, I place some banknotes on the table and tell him I need two shirts.

The following evening the shirts lie folded on the table. One is chequered white like the teacloth, the kind bankers wear, and the other is pink.

The earth was formless and empty

The boy, on schedule to start the day's work, sits at the table and opens the drawing pad. Over the following days he fills one sheet after another with similar drawings, sometimes in black, sometimes in red. The drawing pad follows him between rooms and he gets straight down to work, searches for a table to draw on, hoists himself onto a chair, and begins. The drawings are like the scribbles of a young child, bonfires and sparkling flames. In addition to darkness. In the evenings, he takes the pad up to his room with the black and red pencils. The other colours he leaves behind.

On the fourth day he draws a horizontal line right across the sheet, just above the middle. There can be no doubt that it's a horizon. Then he draws a circle on the upper half of the page, strikingly perfect, as if the child had used a compass. The world is split in two and for that purpose two colours are used, red and black. The sun is ink black and the earth below is ablaze with fire.

Eventually the pencils are reduced to two little black and red stubs, and ultimately just a thread of colour, and finally they're finished. There is no choice but to broaden the palette. The boy gets a new sheet, turns the box of pencils upside down, and contemplates the colours, looking for the right ones. He first chooses blue and draws a small circle. We stand side by side, the mother and the man with the drill, and observe the creation of a newborn world. Then the boy stoops over the drawing again, obstructing our view with his shoulder—he doesn't want to be watched and doesn't look up for a good while because he's too busy with the picture. When he straightens up again, he has drawn four thin lines coming out of the circle. There can be no question that it's a tiny person with arms and legs that he has drawn.

"Me," he says.

"Him," she interprets.

The boy studies the box of pencils, reaches for orange, and immediately starts to draw another circle, bigger than the previous one. He adds four strokes to it, two horizontal and two vertical; another bigger human being is born and fills the sheet.

"Mom" is heard from the table.

To perfect the drawing he adds several smaller strokes, like rays, he counts five fingers on each hand and draws them carefully. He has connected the two people, they're holding hands.

He has created two people, a small man and a big

159

woman, and placed them under a green sun. It's the first day of the world.

And he looked at what he had made *and saw that it was very good*.

His mother smiles at me. The more I try to forget that she is a woman, the more I think about it.

And there was day

The boy is generally never far away.

"Have you seen Adam?" she asks. She is bending over some papers with numbers, accounts, I assume. The boy had been playing near his mom and then suddenly vanished, evaporated.

"He was here a second ago."

She rushes down the corridor. I hear her calling out the boy's name. I put down my screwdriver and follow her.

"There's no point in calling him, he doesn't answer," she says. She opens the door of a cupboard in the corridor.

"He sometimes crawls in here," she says, and adds that the last time she found him behind bundles of clean bed linen and towels.

As we move between rooms, she says she is always afraid of losing Adam. She opens one bedroom door after the next and swiftly scans each room. We also look in the bathrooms and search through wardrobes and under beds.

"He crawls under tables, beds, and vanishes into nooks," his mother explains. "He's always looking for hiding places and I'm so scared he'll get trapped, find some place he can't get out of on his own."

She kneels and looks under the bed.

When she stands up, she brushes down her skirt.

"He's not with Fifi," she says. "I don't get it."

We look on both floors. Finally, she knocks on the door of the man in the leopard socks.

She signals me to wait outside.

"Wait," she says. "I'll do this."

I stand at some distance in the corridor and, after a few moments, the man opens a small slit in the door. I hear her apologise for the inconvenience and ask if he's seen the little boy. Whether he might have come by? They exchange some words and then she disappears into the bedroom, out of my line of view. I hear a conversation and May speaks in fast, hushed tones, but I can't make out what is being said.

After a short while she comes out holding the boy's hand. The edges of his mouth are smudged in brown.

"He was with him," she says with a grave air. "He gave him chocolate," she adds by way of explanation.

And then in a low voice: "Thank you for your help."

She bites her lower lip and confesses she isn't just afraid for Adam, but also for her brother. "Young people like to meet out in the woods and few are willing to go out there to fetch their remains." Those are the words the young woman uses, "young people," like my eighty-three-year-old mother would say.

Once the mother and son have gone back to their room, I knock on my neighbour's door.

"You don't go near that boy," I say.

He looks at me and grins.

"Do you have a crush on the girl? I thought you were getting off with the movie star."

I've no intention of answering him, but he indicates that he has matters to discuss, that he was looking for me, in fact.

Then he immediately gets to the point and asks if I've managed to see the mural.

He doesn't wait for an answer and asks straight out whether I would like to work for him.

"To obtain certain things."

"What things?"

He sips from the glass he is holding in his hands.

"Things you have access to. People trust a person like you, who can bathe in the sunshine of a good conscience."

I am like other people; I love, cry, and suffer

I've become a member of the Hotel Silence staff and have a bunch of keys.

Fifi calls me over and hands me the bundle.

"Since you are now a member of the Hotel Silence staff, we feel you should have the keys."

In return I can stay at the hotel for an unlimited period of time, with breakfast, lunch, and goods from the hotel shop—"while the stock still lasts," as Fifi puts it. I'm also welcome to bring my family later, says May. Fifi makes soup or an omelette at lunchtime, and in the evenings I more often than not go to the restaurant down the road. I have helped the owner with a number of odd jobs and haven't had to pull out my wallet recently. For some reason he hasn't mentioned the swinging doors since last week. When I get back to the hotel, I read. Yesterday I finished *A Cold Spring* by Elizabeth Bishop and started *Fathers and Sons* by Turgenev. I also look in on Fifi in the baths every day and offer him guidance on the tiling.

"It's good to get an outsider's eye," he says. "Maybe I should go to school to learn this properly."

His sister and I take a bedroom a day, and help each other to get them into shape. Then she also needs to take care of her boy.

Sometimes May stops whatever she is doing to watch me work. I also sometimes look up and notice that she is looking at me through the mirror, I observe her observing me. When I look up, she looks away. Or she is on the verge of saying something when she suddenly stops in the middle of a sentence. At times she also looks without seeing, then I know she is thinking of something else. Then she stands

AUÐUR AVA ÓLAFSDÓTTIR

dead still and stares into space with vacant eyes. After some
moments she snaps out of it and says:

"Sorry, I was thinking."

Then there are times when she looks at me like she can't
figure out who I am and is trying to work out where I belong
in her black-and-white world of dust. It comes to a head
when she confronts me for the third time.

I'm helping her to stretch some sheets, we're both tug-
ging in opposite directions and tuck the corners under the
mattress.

"No one comes here on vacation," she says, staring me
in the eye.

I straighten up. I'm standing on one side of the bed and
she on the other.

She wants to know what I'm doing here. Apart from
helping her with the sheets.

If we were to sit down, me and this young woman in
pink plimsolls, and compare our scars, our maimed bodies,
and count how many stitches had been sewn from the neck
down and then draw a line between them and add them all
up, she would be the winner. My scratches are insignificant,
laughable. Even if I had lance wounds in my side, the girl
would win the prize.

"No one travels here without some purpose," she repeats.

The same thing the man in the socks said.

I haven't spotted him for several days. Didn't he say he
had some business to attend to in the country?

"The world is full of men like you who misunderstand life," he'd said to me the last time I bumped into him.

Even I was beginning to doubt my purpose.

Before I know it, I've said it.

"I actually came to die."

She looks straight at me.

"Are you ill or . . .?"

"No."

I sense she wants more information.

"To die how?"

"To kill myself. I haven't decided how yet."

"I understand."

I don't know what she understands.

Should I mention that there are people in this world who want to die because they can't bear what happens anymore? That would be the longest sentence I'd have uttered in two weeks.

"Why didn't you just stay at home?"

She doesn't ask whether it wouldn't be better to die surrounded by cold mountains.

"I wanted to protect my daughter from discovering me."

"And not me?" she asks. "You don't want to protect me?"

"Forgive me," I say. "I didn't know you would be here. Or the boy. I didn't expect to meet you. I didn't know you then," I add, feeling the triviality of every word I utter.

I can't tell this young woman, who owns nothing but life itself, that I'm lost. Or that life turned out to be different than what I expected. If I were to say: I'm like other people, I love, cry, and suffer, she would probably understand me and say: I know what you mean.

"I was unhappy," I say.

That's the second time I mention that, if I include Mom.

"I didn't know how to fix it," I add.

I can almost hear Mom's voice. "All suffering is unique and different," she said once, "and therefore it can't be compared. Happiness, on the other hand, is similar."

May stares at the floor.

"Adam's father was an economist who played in a jazz band. Adam was born in the basement of a stranger's house and I was alone there with his father. We both cried. Such a beautiful angel who had fallen from the sky, his father said."

She falls silent, walks over to the window and then continues. Searches for words and chooses them carefully:

"He was shot out on the football pitch and we couldn't reach him. Not even to collect the body because he lay in a fighting zone. We didn't get to hold him, wash him, bury him. We saw him through binoculars, the trickles of blood down his trouser legs and jacket sleeves. We thought he was dead, but the next day he had changed position. At first he lay on his back and the next day he lay on his side, in the evening he had crawled two metres towards the goalposts. I would never have believed so much blood could come from one person. It took him three days to die. After that he lay still and we watched him shrivel into his clothes until we were forced to flee and leave him behind."

"Forgive me," I say again.

Should I tell her I don't understand myself, would that not just make it worse?

She is sitting on the chair and I walk to her and sit beside her.

"Sorrow is like a piece of glass in the throat," she says.

"I'm not going to die. Not immediately," I say.

I could just as well have said, don't worry because I don't know how to die. No more than Mom can. Or I could say to this girl, who has looked down the barrels of so many guns and survived, that I'm not the same man I was ten days ago. Or yesterday. That I'm in a state of flux.

"Dad, did you know that the body's cells renew themselves every seven years," Waterlily had said.

"Yes, isn't a man constantly in the act of becoming? Always being renewed?" Svanur had asked down at the harbour, by the choppy green ocean, with the whale-watching boats on one side of the pier and the whale-hunting boats on the other.

"We're born, love, suffer, and die," I hear her say with a long sniff.

"I know," I say.

"Some of my friends didn't get a chance to try love," she continues. "Only to suffer and die."

I nod.

"Even if we didn't know if we were going to get shot today or tomorrow, we never stopped loving."

She is standing again, by the window with her back turned to me. Her tight blouse clinging to her shoulders.

"We kept the boat afloat, all three of us, Fifi, Adam, and I. We wanted to live, if not then we'd die together. So no one would be left behind."

The boy, who has been sitting at the table fitting the pearls onto the pink heart that I found in the hotel shop, now slides off the chair and positions himself beside his mother. He offers her his hand and they stand side by side with their backs turned to me. He understands she is upset. He looks at his mother and then over his shoulder at me. And then again. I hear him say something with a questioning tone. He wants an answer. He wants to know what's going on.

"Did you know that blood turns black when it hardens?" she finally says, continuing to fix her gaze on the ocean.

Should I tell her that she can take refuge under my wings while she's waiting for the light to reappear?

I walk over to her and say:

"You've done really well."

She turns, but doesn't let go of the boy's hand, the sun is behind her and she stands in the middle of a radiant cloud of shimmering dust.

"We try to do our best," she says. "As people."

Flood calls unto flood

The word has spread that I'm helping out the siblings and I've received several enquiries and requests from other people in the town, mainly women, wanting assistance with this or that. The queries have multiplied over the past few days and this morning there were five messages waiting in the lobby. Fifi says he took the liberty to write down orders and hands me some folded notes. Most of the jobs concern red water in the taps, clogged sinks, leaking seals, broken cookers, and other domestic appliances.

I know where the residual-current device is, but there is a shortage of spare parts: tubes, wires, cans, washers.

Can I fix a washing machine? Know anything about computers? A mirror also has to be put up on the other side of town.

I do what I'm asked to do so long as it doesn't send me down into the sewage system with a torch.

"Hi, Mister Fix," it says in the first folded letter. That's what they call me.

"People say you can fix anything," the young man explains. "They also call you Mister Miracle."

"They're wrong on that account," I say to him. "Besides, they're only temporary repairs," I add.

My insistence on the fact that I'm neither a plumber nor an electrician falls on deaf ears. They need an electrician. They need a carpenter. They need plumbers. They need builders.

"There are so few people who know anything about electricity," says Fifi.

"Some people think it's not fair that you're only helping women," I hear him add without looking at me. "I just wanted you to know that. And one other thing, there was a call from the restaurant. I'm supposed to tell you they're serving blood pudding this evening."

RED

I pluck up the courage to remind May of the need for paint, even though I suspect it's difficult to come by.

"The rooms need painting."

She puts down the vacuum cleaner.

"Just not red."

Since the walls that don't have any leafy wallpaper on them are light blue, her comment is bewildering.

I suggest they stick to the same colour.

"Don't you want to keep the same colour?"

"There was blood all over the country. Every footstep was bloody, there were pools of blood on the streets. Blood streamed down the roads, it was raining blood, and in the end all the rivers were red with blood," she says in a detached voice, as if she were delivering a lecture, staring at the light blue wall as she speaks.

"We poured red paint into the cracks the bombs left in the asphalt so that it would form blood roses. So there's no red paint left in the country," she concludes.

I remain silent.

"There might be some filler," she says, turning to me again, "but you need the right connections to get paint."

She stands dead still in the middle of the floor and takes a deep breath before continuing:

"Human flesh is so delicate, the skin so quick to tear, steel bullets rip organs to shreds, concrete smashes bones, glass severs limbs," she rattles off with a glazed expression.

"There, there," I say, as if I were talking to a child who's afraid of the dark.

"It's such a short way to the heart," she says.

"There, there," I say, taking her into my arms. The door is open to the corridor.

It's then that I notice that the boy is standing in the door-way and staring at us alternately. He had popped down to his uncle to hand him the tiles and to have a go at stirring the plaster and now he's returned. I let go of her and turn away. Even though I've little sense of myself, I can feel the outlines of another living body.

The boy rushes over to his mother.

I'm about to say something else but instead ask:

"Where is that house you're going to move into, you women?" On several occasions she has mentioned a house that she and some of her female friends were going to renovate and live in together. Seven women, if I remember correctly, with three children. And Fifi.

She looks at me. Eyeing me like a stranger. Which I am to myself and to others.

"If you like, I could take a look at it for you," I continue.

She is silent for a long moment.

"You're lucky you haven't killed anyone," she finally says.

HOUSE OF WOMEN

The house stands on the other side of the town centre, and on our way May explains to me that the women who are going to live there together have been roaming from place to place and are staying in temporary accommodations at the moment. They have nothing, just a suitcase each or less.

"One of them has papers that say she owns the house and she has invited the others to live with her. So there'll be seven women and three children living there," she confirms. "And then there's Fifi," she adds. "That'll make two men, a twenty-year-old and a five-year-old, an uncle and a nephew who have both survived the war."

She tells me that some of the women are going to help run the hotel when the tourists return.

The house is a three-storey building that stands on its own at the top of the street; the houses on either side of it were blown up. It has a big uncultivated lawn and creeping ivy that stretches to the top floor. May says that the cousin of one of the women was supposed to be helping out with the repairs, but he hasn't been heard from in a long time.

"I think it's fairly likely that he's left the country," she concludes.

The garden has high walls and I see how a play area could be made for the children. Even though most of the windows of the house are broken, at first glance, the foundation seems to be in a good state. The walls are in one piece and the flooring in surprisingly fine condition, but there's no running water in the house, no electricity, and no heating. The water pipes and drainage are at the bottom of the neighbourhood and the main worry is that the house has been excluded from the new town planning.

"We're struggling to get it included," says May.

There is no furniture in the house, but judging by the mattress on the floor in one of the bedrooms, it's obvious that someone has been staying here. I see that it will be possible to fix up the house, but I'll need more tools and materials. The pipes, sewage system, and electrical wiring also need mending. With some minor illegal adjustments we could temporarily connect to the electricity grid and start on some of the most pressing tasks. First the house needs to be sealed off from rodents and rain and the windowpanes have to be changed. I conduct an inspection and see that the mullions and window frames are intact.

"I really want to help you—you women," I say. "I can do some things but not everything."

May and I are on the second floor of the house and I'm finishing the measurements of a window when I sense something weighing on her.

"There is one thing I wanted to mention to you before you meet the other women," she says, leaning against a wall. "The thing is," she says, "just like we don't talk about who did what, we don't ask about who went through what either."

"I understand."

I sense some agitation in her.

"You don't ask a man if he's killed someone or a woman if she has been raped or by how many."

"No, you don't have to worry about me asking any questions," I say.

"And when one sees a child, one doesn't wonder whether it's the child of a woman who was raped by an enemy soldier."

"No, one doesn't."

She adjusts a lock of hair, tucks it under the clip.

"All women are subjected to violence in war," she continues without looking at me.

I think of how young she is and how much she's been through.

"Soldiers don't knock on your door to ask for your permission to shoot."

"No, they don't."

She adjusts her hair again.

"The only way to continue is to pretend we lead a normal life. To pretend everything is okay. To shut one's eyes to the destruction."

I notice she has small pearl earrings that she touches from time to time, as if to reassure herself that they're in place.

I mention this to her and tell her they're beautiful.

"From my mother," she says, and is about to add something but stops.

She hesitates.

"Despite the fear, I still clearly remember the stars at night. And the moon too, yes."

I mention the state where all lose themselves, the good and the bad

When I get back to the hotel, I rip out the last page in the diary and make a list of what has to be done in the house and what I need.

I'd caught a glimpse of my neighbour in the corridor and know he's back. I knock on the door of number nine.

When he opens, I hand him the list without accepting an invitation to step inside.

He says it could well be that he knows contractors who are building in the area. The question is what would he get in return.

"Nothing."

"Nothing? That's not how it works. I do you a favour and you do me a favour in return."

"Not in this case. You'll do things and get nothing in return. Except satisfaction," I add.

"You've got to follow the rules of the game."

"No, you've got to tell the contractors, your friends, that otherwise they'll have the women against them."

This takes him by surprise.

"Am I to tell the contractors, my friends, that otherwise they'll have the women against them?"

He repeats my words. I take that as a sign that he's thinking. Then he says:

"The house hasn't been included in the reconstruction plan. It may be that some people don't want you poking your nose into what they're doing. Are you going to fix the whole country? Armed with your little drill and measuring tape? Do you think you can glue back together a broken world?"

As he says this, I suddenly remember the floral dish with a gilded rim that I broke as a child and glued back together again. It took a lot of work to get the fragments to fit, but I succeeded. Which was why I was surprised when Mom threw it away some days later.

"The world won't be good just because you've got a roll of Sellotape," I hear him say.

EXCHANGE OF MESSAGES

Two days later there is a message waiting for me in reception. The young man hands me a folded handwritten note: *Work on sewage system has commenced.*

In the next message, I send him the measurements of the windows and the glass I need.

The answer comes the next day:

Goods will be delivered on Monday.

I can then start working on the windows.

We write to each other for a whole week.

Floor materials have arrived.

The last message reads: *Area has been swept for mines (garden safe).*

NOLI ME TANGERE
(TOUCH ME NOT)

Adam is with Fifi in the baths, helping him to sort through the body parts and search for three missing breasts, and I'm moving a wardrobe with May when she asks me:

"Are you married?"

"No, divorced."

"Do you have any other children apart from the daughter you mentioned the other day?"

177

"No."

"How old is she?"

"Twenty-six."

Before I know it, I've told her that Waterlily isn't mine.

"My daughter isn't exactly mine," I say.

By way of explanation, I add:

"I'm not her blood father."

I think about those words: blood father.

"Have you been alone for long?"

"Six months."

If she'd asked have I been lonely for long, I would have answered eight years and five months.

That is precisely what she asks about next, loneliness.

"Aren't you lonely?"

"Sometimes."

She edges closer to me, is almost standing right against me.

"Don't you long to feel the warmth of another body?"

I'm silent and then say:

"It's been such a long time."

"How long?"

"Pretty long."

"More than two years?"

Should I trust her with this?

I take a deep breath before saying it:

"Eight years and five months." I could have added eleven days.

She slides against me and I feel her closeness grow like a full moon.

Should I tell her how things are, that I don't know how to do it anymore?

That I'm scared?

I hesitate.

"You're my daughter's age."

"I'm older than her," she says. "I'm older than you. I'm two hundred years old and I've seen it all. Besides, I thought she wasn't yours, your daughter."

"No, but she's still my daughter." I could have added, "She's the only Gudrún Waterlily Jónasdóttir in the whole world."

"But I'm not her."

My heart pounds.

"No, you're not her."

I try to think fast.

"What about younger men, of your age?"

"They don't exist. I wake up and look at the man lying on the pillow beside me and think he's killed somebody. Still, that wasn't why I asked," she adds softly.

What can I say?

That I'm not the man for her. That she'll know him when he comes because he will have forged a ploughshare from a sword. And then I would start working on the tiling as if nothing had happened.

"I need more time," I say.

"How much time?"

It's not that the question isn't an important one, just that I don't know the answer.

A man is half man, half animal

There is a stew with some kind of meat and noodles at Restaurant Limbo. I detect a taste of paprika and cumin and pull the bay leaf out of the mash and place it on the rim of the bowl. The owner immediately drags over a chair to chat and says that he's heard I've been helping women in the town with various odd jobs. He lists off sinks, TVs, aerials, washing machines.

"It's the talk of the town," he says. "We've also heard that you've thrown yourself into fixing up a house."

He is quiet for a moment and assumes a grave air:

"These things get around."

"Yes, they asked me for help," I say.

I could have added, a woman asks me to do something and I do it.

I'm used to that from home.

"It can cause problems."

"Yeah?"

"Yeah, it doesn't look good. That you only help women. It doesn't go down too well. Some people are offended by it."

He has the expression of a man who is about to burst into tears.

He pauses in his speech, to give himself time to recover.

"Yes, there are also men in this world who need help. There has to be an equal share," he says. And then adds, "Even though some people don't realise it."

He stands up to take the bowl and says that he had actually intended to offer me some almond cake. He stresses the words "had actually intended to" as if he'd given up on the idea. Because there is no longer any reason for it.

"While I've been cooking for you, almost every day, you still refuse to make those swinging doors."

I'd forgotten them.

"I've discussed them with you several times."

He stands with the bowl in his hands and doesn't seem to be on his way to the kitchen anymore.

"I got you shirts and you say you can't manage one set of swinging doors."

I reflect on this.

"Didn't we need some materials?"

"I've got them."

"Including the hinges?"

"Yes, including the hinges."

"And tools?"

"I'm working on them."

I tell him I also want to be remunerated:

"I want to be paid."

181

He throws up his arms.

"You'll be paid in meals. Free meals. Once a day."

I think about how much he needs me and what demands I can make. Barter is the only currency around here. I tell him I'll make the swinging doors if I get to keep the tools:

"I want to be paid in tools," I say.

And I turn over the menu and make sketches.

"I need both a normal saw and a jigsaw," I say.

Screws

Chisels in two widths

Sandpaper

Filler

Brushes and scrapers

He has sat down at the table in front of me and is making out his list too. There are a few things that need to be checked out at Restaurant Limbo.

"And," I add, "I want to be able to choose the menu. Not just birds and stew. No more pigeons."

Afterwards he wants to seal the deal with a shot.

The sun is red and sinking when I return to the hotel.

That night I dream there's a rat on the loose in the bedroom.

The floor is covered in scraps of wood and I recognise fragments of furniture from my and Gudrún's home, including the adjustable stool I made.

Virility is
to kill an adult animal

I was longer than I had planned working on the windows on the top floor of the women's house and soon the curfew begins. It's getting dark and before long the moon will be the only source of light. I check to see if I can spot the moon and whether it's in its place.

All of a sudden I get the feeling that I'm not alone, that someone is watching me, and I think I hear footsteps, but not so much footsteps as becoming aware of a big silent shadow vanishing behind the corner ahead of me. An animal comes to mind. A big cat. What species did the actress say had escaped from the municipal zoo?

I'm close to the square of the hotel and pause to scan my surroundings, but spot nothing, neither animal nor man. Not a soul in sight.

A figure promptly materialises in front of me and seems to be in a rush. I can't work out which is bigger, the moon or the man, whether it is rising or he is drawing closer, it rushes into the clouds and he heads straight for me. As soon as he comes up to me, he utters something I can't understand. Was it a question or a statement? Before I get a chance to answer, I feel a swift blow and, a moment later, I'm lying in the street. And I feel another blow and red rain pouring over me. Something hot and wet trickles down my temples. The man looms above me like

183

a lunar eclipse, or tank, and kicks me. I smell the scent of aftershave and leather. I think, should I defend myself or count myself into the night? Then, just as quickly, he has stopped beating me and I hear footsteps moving away and see the glow of a cigarette like a blip in the middle of the moon. Then I hear a scooter being kick-started. There's a taste of blood in my mouth but I feel an odd contentment. Something furry and familiar rubs against my shoulder as I lie in the street; it figures, it's the cat from the restaurant, the one-eyed cat. I stretch out my bleeding hand to stroke him, a burst of black particles swirl around my eyes.

I clamber to my feet. I hear footsteps again, someone running towards me from the hotel.

"Mister Jónas," I hear an anxious voice call out. It's Fifi who rushes over and grabs me under the arm. I feel cold, but manage to remain totally lucid in my thoughts:

If the actress asks me to sleep with her when she comes back from her journey, I'll say yes without hesitation. It's been more than a week and she hasn't returned yet.

FOUR

Four stern faces look down at me, inspecting me: May, Fifi, the boy, and an unknown woman.

I've already vomited once and I have to vomit again.

"You've suffered a blow to your head and a concussion, and we have to stitch that cut on your forehead," says the woman, pulling out a syringe. Out of a toolbox.

"A few stitches," she adds.

I catch a whiff of orange peel and when I turn my head I see the boy standing close to the bed, holding a slice of orange, he's wearing a T-shirt that reads "Stockholm I love you." Taking another step forward, he presses himself right against the edge of the bed and lifts the blanket that someone has spread over me, to conduct an examination. I try to remember; it was Fifi who dragged me to my room.

"Hi," I say, trying to smile at the boy.

His mother says something to him and he lets go of the blanket. Then she looks at me, she's upset and has tears in her eyes.

"What happened?" she asks. "Who attacked you?"

I think I answer her but can't be sure.

"It's okay," I say.

I am like molten rock. *I'm like other people, I suffer,* I wrote in my diary when I was twenty-one years old. In the sentence above I had written: *Full moon. Three degrees.*

When I stand, it's not just my head that pulsates but the whole room, revolving. I spin, I feel as if I'm looking at the earth from the peak of a mountain, outlines vibrate and slowly shimmer, as if under plexiglass.

I stagger to the bathroom to throw up.

185

When I lie down again, the unknown woman bends over me and shines a light in my eyes. She tells me to unbutton my shirt so she can examine me, while May gathers her brother and son, drawing them back into a corner of the room. They stand in a cluster, observing.

The woman asks disjointed questions: what my name is, how old I am, and asks me to count my fingers. I have five on one hand and five on the other, unlike many others in this town.

"Are you married?"

"Yes," I say. "Or to be precise, no."

I sit topless on the edge of the bed.

"Are you married or not?"

"Not anymore. Divorced."

"Do you have any children?"

"Yes. Or no. I have a daughter, but I don't."

She continues unfazed.

"When is your birthday?"

I feel as if I'm looking at them and the bedroom in disjointed freeze-frames, jamming and hopping from one to the next, waiting for the film to start running smoothly again.

"May twenty-fifth."

The woman looks at May and she looks at her brother. They look at each other.

"That's today," says the woman.

I reach for my passport and hand it to them, it's passed around. I notice how they scrutinise it and turn the pages.

What should I do about this? Invite them to a birthday party?

"You're bruised but nothing's broken, so from that point of view you're lucky," she says when she's finished examining me. "You can button up your shirt."

Then she nods at me as she's packing her bag.

"Nice flower."

MOM

"You spoke about your mother," May says. "Before the doctor came in. You said, Mom. I understood it. You repeated the word."

When I look at her questioningly, she adds:

"One doesn't have to understand everything that is said to understand."

I ask her what day it is.

"Is it Monday?"

"No."

"Tuesday?"

"No. Wednesday."

"How long have I been here?"

"Three weeks."

I stand up and ask her if there is a male choir in the town. She's bewildered.

187

"Yes," she says hesitantly. "I think they're short of voices. Tenors mainly, I think."

"I must call my daughter," I say.

"Are you going back home?"

"Not yet. I have some things to finish."

She smiles.

Then she remembers something.

"By the way," she says, "the house has been connected to the water supply. Water started spurting into the sink. So things are looking up."

If I were to ask her what she dreams about, what would she answer? Of light springing on the horizon again?

A man only dies once

They let me use the phone at the reception desk.

It takes a few seconds for Waterlily to answer:

"Is that you, Dad? Is everything okay?"

"Yes, everything is fine."

Her voice is tearful and she says she's been beside herself with worry since she found the letter and I disappeared.

"It was impossible to get hold of you."

She says she found my mobile phone on the bedside table, and the wardrobe in the bedroom was empty.

"Yes, I gave away the clothes."

I hesitate and add:

"I didn't need them anymore."

I try to remember the letter and what I'd written. She enlightens me:

"You said you were going on a journey without saying where or for how long."

She says I'm inarticulate and once more asks if everything is okay. Where am I exactly? What am I doing and when am I coming home? Did I get into some trouble? I hear she's fighting back the tears.

"Mom is worried too," she adds.

My voice wavers when I ask:

"Really, was Mom worried too?"

"Yeah, Mom too. She's not indifferent to you," she adds after a moment's hesitation.

She says she received the postcard yesterday, with a picture of a mosaic wall and the name of a hotel, but that no one answered at the phone number she found online. She adds that she and her mother are not happy about the fact that I chose to go to the most dangerous country in the world.

"Not anymore. The war is over."

She rephrases it:

"Well, certainly one of the most dangerous countries in the world."

I hear her blowing her nose.

"Isn't everything in ruins?"

"Yes."

"And land mines everywhere?"

189

"Yes, that too."

Should she catch a plane? Can she come to me?

There is silence at the other end of the line. Has she started to cry?

I take a deep breath before I say it:

"Your Mom says you're not mine. She had a boyfriend when we met."

I could have added, just before we went on the mountain hike on which you should have been conceived. With ptarmigans, a sheep, and the mountain as our witnesses.

"After the mountain, there was no one else but you," Gudrún had said.

"Yes, I know. At first I was angry, but now it doesn't matter. I've got no other dad but you."

"And the other one?"

"Am I to swap dads after twenty-six years? Are you really going to disown me? And abandon me?"

There's silence on the phone.

"Is that why you went away?" she then asks. I say nothing.

"Why is there so much money in my bank account?"

"I sold Steel Legs Ltd." And add: "I'm trying to simplify my life."

"I suspected something was up when you asked me whether I was happy," she says finally.

Before I realise it, I hear myself saying:

"I'm going to extend my stay. I've got a job."

"Job?"

"Yes, sort of. It'll delay me. For several weeks."

"Several weeks?"

"Yes, I'm helping some women here to fix up a house."

"Some women?"

Now she's the one repeating what I say.

"There's a girl here the same age as you. She has a young son."

"Does she have a crush on you?"

I hesitate.

"I'm not sure. Maybe."

"And you, do you have a crush on her?"

"Like I said, she's your age. A few years older," I add.

"You haven't answered my question."

"No, it's not like that. There's a shortage of handy men who own drills."

"Did you take it with you? The drill?"

"Yes."

Silence.

Then I say:

"I feel a responsibility."

It's as if I could hear Svanur's voice: "He who knows and does nothing is the guilty one."

I can hear her breathing, so she hasn't hung up.

She is still on the line.

"Do you remember, Dad, when we lay on our tummies over the frozen lake and looked down at the vegetation below the ice?"

191

"Yes, I remember that."

"Promise you'll phone."

"Promise."

"Happy birthday, Dad," she says finally.

Few men kill, most just die

I see from a streak of light in the corridor that the man's door is open. He's in a dressing gown and waiting for me.

"There's no point in getting the police involved in the case" is the first thing he says to me when I stagger down the corridor after finishing the green pea soup Fifi cooked for me.

The world keeps on turning.

Still.

He says this nonchalantly, as if he were talking to himself.

"Aren't you curious to know why you weren't killed?"

"No."

"They thought you were someone else."

I don't ask who else, nor do I tell him that it's quite possible I may be someone other than who I am. That I don't know where I end or begin.

"Were you afraid of dying?"

"No."

"No, you're the type of person who would rather be killed than kill. You're not the kind of guy who has grazed knuckles at the end of a fight."

192

I don't bother answering him.

He continues:

"If you should have been killed, you would have been killed."

One man is no competition for a contractor. A man with a drill doesn't stand a chance against a bulldozer.

"Has the sewage system been sorted?"

"They can thank you for that, the ladies."

He changes the subject.

"Apart from that I quite like you. Per se."

He knows Latin.

"But I immediately saw that you were in some kind of trouble, in too much of a hurry to get away from yourself, a man with no luggage, we all know what that means."

The order of things

I quickly browse through the last diary. At the back there are several scattered, undated sentences. One per page:

Is it true that the year 525 immediately followed the year 241?

And two pages later, I wrote:

Not everything happens in the right order.

This is followed by several blank pages. And then this sentence:

Everything can happen. It can also be different than what one expected.

In the evening there is a knock on the door, low down. Adam stands outside, followed closely by his mother.

May is holding a cake and presents it with a smile.

"Happy birthday, Mister Jónas," says the boy.

"He's been practicing," she says.

I have drawn the blinds on the windows but the sun squeezes through the gaps and forms an elongated box on the floor, a white patch of light that falls on the tiles.

The boy hands me a drawing that depicts three trees with large crowns and orange peaks surmounted by a green sky.

"A forest," the mother interprets.

They stand in the middle of the light, the mother and son, directly above the maze.

Clouds crash-landing
salty tears

I wake up with a headache and pain all over my body. The bedsheet is pasted to me and I feel strangely clammy, my skin tingles with goose bumps, as if it had suddenly been covered with highly sensitive receptors to the world.

I wander into the bathroom and look into the mirror. My face is swollen and bloated and starting to darken around the eyes.

I turn on the shower and stand under the warm jet until the hot water runs out. The water is blood-tinted at first. I grope my body, joints, shoulders, wrists, knees, collarbone. I have a nasty scratch on my side, lacerations and cuts on my palms. When I've finished washing, I pluck the stones out of my hands, tiny pebbles the size of peas, I put on my pink shirt in honour of the day, and step out onto the balcony. The heavens have sunk and opened. I stretch out my hands and turn the palms up to the sky—there is a white band around the finger on my left hand where I used to wear my wedding ring—then I slowly raise my hands to the heavens and allow the rain to pour onto my wounds and the pink shirt, which clings to my water lily.

I have a body.

I am my body.

Suddenly a transparent butterfly flutters towards me, perches on my arm and folds its silver wings, it's huge. The rain pitter-patters on the balcony. And I think to myself, the women's house is rain-proof now. I changed the last window the day before yesterday.

Words have consequences

Fifi is standing outside the bedroom door with a box of books in his arms, wearing a cap backwards.

"I thought you might like to have the rest," he says, "instead of having to go down to the basement every time you want a new book."

He puts the box down in the middle of the floor.

"You can calmly and slowly go through them while you're recovering," he adds.

I tell him I'm almost better.

He looks at me with great scepticism.

"Not that I can see."

He reaches into the box and pulls out a book.

"There's a phrase book to learn the language, which you might be interested in. I recommend it. Obviously no one speaks Icelandic here and not everyone speaks English either." I open the book and see that it's designed to help tourists get by in various circumstances, such as ordering in a restaurant, buying a train ticket or stamps at the post office, asking for the route out of the woods. The pronunciation of the words is written in brackets at the end of each sentence. I browse through the pages. There is a special chapter called "Troubleshooting," which, among other things, includes the following phrase:

I'm lost. How can I get back to my hotel?

And similarly:

Please wait a moment while I search for a phrase in this book.

I skim ahead and see that on the last page it says:

It was all a misunderstanding, I'm very sorry.

Further on there is a chapter called "Things That Sometimes Get Lost," which includes an exhaustive list:

Raincoat

Gloves

Scarf

Umbrella
Glasses
Wedding ring
Passport
Pen
Screwdriver

It doesn't say anything about one's self, I say to myself.

I reckon I can learn five new phrases per day.

In a week's time, I'd have thirty-five phrases. How many words does one need to survive?

It's as if I could hear Mom: "Words can be misunderstood in so many ways. Look at your father, for example."

Fifi says he has been gathering information, but no one knows exactly who attacked me.

"Some people thought you were working for a man—called Williams," he says. The information is confusing and contradictory. There has also been mention of the women I've been working for. For free. Some people are dissatisfied about that, as had been pointed out to me the other day.

"They feel it's not fair," he repeats.

Finally, he heard that I provoked the assailant by looking him in the eye—right into his pupils—when I met him.

"We don't do that here," he says.

"We do that where I come from," I say.

We look into the eyes of the people we meet on the street. Otherwise we don't know whether we're supposed to greet them or not.

197

Before Fifi leaves, he digs into the breast pocket of his chequered shirt and pulls out a pair of sunglasses.

"These are from the storage room," he says, handing them to me. I try them on.

The price tag is still on.

"Pilot," he says. "To shield your swollen eyes." He hesitates.

"I can't read books anymore," I hear him say. "When I was a boy I read a lot, but then I stopped with the war."

He hesitates again.

"It takes only one sentence to blow up a village. Two sentences to destroy the world."

He doesn't say I've seen it all, my father with a bullet hole in his head and my sister's son being born in a musty basement.

He adjusts his cap.

And another thing, yes. He found four boxes of spare tiles in the ancient baths and was wondering if I could use them in the house I'm fixing up for the women.

"That house is also for you," I say. "And for Adam."

"Yes, that you're fixing for the women, me, and Adam."

I still exist
I'm still here

I open the diary and rapidly skim through densely written pages until I reach blank sheets at the back. I leave a gap of one page after the last entry, which I made some twenty-seven years ago: *She will survive me*. Next I grab the pen with "Hotel Silence" inscribed on it and at the top of the page write the date: *29 May*. Followed by: *For Waterlily*.

I know I can choose among thirty-three letters, which is more than in most other languages. I start with two sentences:

I still exist.

I'm still here.

And then add another:

I'm trying to understand why.

What more can I write? Should I describe the sky, say that I wake up at night and that black trees wrestle with the black sky, that the moon is bigger than it is back home, that I have started to look at myself in the mirror? That I read poetry? That half of what I eat are things I've never eaten before?

I take a moment, then continue:

The water is as red as when a bloody shirt is rinsed in a bathtub.

That's a total of fifteen words.

I add another three words: *Everything dusty grey.*

And then a whole sentence in the line below:

Yesterday for dinner there were big potatoes with the meat (like the ones that your granny boils with goulash), grown in fields where there are no land mines.

Finally:

Need screws?

Cross that out:

~~Need screws?~~

I skip the spare parts.

All of a sudden May is standing at the door and she asks what I'm writing.

"Are you writing a story?" she asks.

"You could say that."

"What happens?"

"I haven't decided it all yet."

"Does someone die?"

"Only the old people. Everyone dies in the right age sequence."

"Good."

She puts down a towel.

"I don't fear the night anymore," I hear her say as she closes the door behind her.

I wait for the world
to take on a form

Fifi informs me that someone is asking for me downstairs.

It's the owner of the restaurant, who has turned up with my thuggish assailant. The men have positioned themselves by the sunglasses stand. I also notice that an inflatable tiger has been added to the hotel shop since yesterday.

"It was a misunderstanding" is the first thing the restaurant owner says.

The thug remains silent. He's wearing a leather jacket over a patterned shirt and has an earring in one ear.

The owner pushes him aside.

"He says he's sorry," he continues. The brute has a sullen expression that betrays no sign of remorse.

"He's not going to do it again."

"That's good to hear."

"He wants to show you something. You need to follow him."

Should I follow my assailant? Follow him down a twisted alley?

"No, I'm in no mood for that."

"You won't regret it. He wants to make up for this misunderstanding."

"No, I'm not interested." And I add that I'm busy. Which happens to be true. I'm reading Dorothy Parker's biography, *What Fresh Hell Is This?*

"He's going to get furniture for the house you're working on. You said the women needed furniture."

I mull on this. We need furniture for three floors, seven women, three children, and one brother.

"What do you say about that?" he continues.

"Nothing."

"Would you be willing to consider it?"

The restaurant owner drags me over to the fireplace. We stand by the forest landscape painting, or under it, to be precise; from this perspective, the light falls on the canvas

201

differently and I notice that the tree trunks in the foreground of the picture are withered on one side.

"You've demonstrated that you are a real man," he says, slapping a hand on my shoulder.

He nods towards the thug. As far as I can make out, he's trying out sunglasses in the mirror. Fifi is keeping an eye on him but also keeps us in view.

"He said you weren't afraid."

I think quickly. My head is still full of stitches.

"A man must forgive," says the restaurant owner, and adds that what they're talking about is a warehouse, full of furniture, which is about to be torn down to build a pharmaceutical factory. It so happens that he knows the contractor supervising the project. The furniture has piled up in the warehouse, rescued from here and there when ruins were being cleared or abandoned houses were emptied. It contains more or less a full inventory of household items.

"My acquaintance needs to get rid of it before the bulldozer drives over it. You're welcome to take anything you want. It would have been quickest to set it all on fire, but the contractor didn't get the permit from the town," he concludes.

He lowers his voice and takes me by the arm.

"I've heard there's some fine bits of furniture between the piles. Quality stuff. Recliners with footrests."

I give it some thought. I see that my assailant is looking in the mirror with a price tag dangling between his eyes.

"Nine o'clock tomorrow morning," I say. "On the dot."

CHOIR BOY

The assailant shows up punctually at nine and waits in the lobby. The top four buttons of his shirt are undone, flashing his tanned chest, and he's wearing the mirrored sunglasses that he bought the day before and doesn't remove, despite the dim light. Fifi seems apprehensive and asks to come with us, but I decline the offer and follow the thug.

The warehouse is located on the outskirts of the town, and on the way my escort repeats that this has all been a misunderstanding.

I'm in no mood to discuss the issue and point out that, if he wants to talk to me, he'll have to take off his sunglasses.

He immediately complies.

"Call me Bingo," he says.

When he pulls back the sliding door of the warehouse, it turns out to be crammed with furniture and personal items that have been thrown together haphazardly.

Entire lives, I think to myself.

"The place has been combed for explosives," he says before we step inside.

The warehouse looks like something between a flea market and a furniture storage room and, surprisingly, most of its contents seem to be in decent enough shape. Other things can be fixed or modified. It's no problem to make some legs for a tabletop or to revamp furniture, that's where I'm on home ground.

"People have been using this as firewood," he says, pushing aside half a chest of drawers.

Should I tell him I don't feel like talking? That I'd be grateful to spend this time together in silence?

I need furniture for three floors and start collecting items for the bottom floor. I drag out a teak dining table and two armchairs and start looking for chairs to fit the table.

"I need a moving van," I say, fishing out another table, a desk lamp, and a standing lamp. I mentally count the number of beds that are needed and try to imagine where the furniture could go.

Bingo says he can get a van and a buddy to assist with the carrying.

He helps me move wardrobes and a crib for the infant in the group to the entrance. There I gather the furniture. I only have to say the word and he does it for me without question. It's obvious that he is used to obeying orders. I manage to find beds for all the occupants of the house, although the mattresses are ruined and need to be found somewhere else. On the other hand, May had said she could get some old but decent enough duvet covers at the hotel, which she was going to take with her to the house. I step between the items and point: this, this, and this. Yes, that desk and that swivelling chair over there. I also pick up a few bicycles.

Bingo lifts up a birdcage and I shake my head.

"There's stuff there from apartments that foreigners left behind when they fled the country," says my henchman, who is now sitting in an armchair with his feet on a table. I notice a valuable antique chair, but don't bother telling him. I signal him to stand up.

I'm at the very back of the warehouse searching for another wardrobe when I spot a patterned rug that has been thrown over something. When I lift it, I discover a stack of tins of paint. I inspect them and see that they are unopened.

Bingo follows me, flabbergasted.

"That must be from some building supplies store, stock that ended up here," he concludes. "If we'd known, we could have sold it."

He pulls out a penknife and prises open one of the tins.

I pick out the tins and open them, one by one.

"This one, this one, and this one," I say, and he stacks them by the furniture.

I search for varnish.

"I need sandpaper, brushes, and varnish," I say.

That way I could start working on the floors next week.

He gets down on all fours and rummages through the stock of tins, moving his lips as he reads the labels. Meanwhile, I grab four rolls of leaf-patterned wallpaper.

As we're leaving and Bingo is about to slide the door closed, I spot a record player just by the entrance. It's on the floor under a table and, at first glance, seems to be undamaged. I lift the lid and examine the needle. Despite five years of warfare, air raids, melted asphalt, and shredded flesh, the needle seems to be intact. I look around. It figures, a few feet away lies a box with a substantial vinyl collection. I quickly browse through the records, which include some fine recordings with Maria Callas and Jussi Björling. There's Franz Liszt's *Dance of the Dead* and Rachmaninoff's *Rhapsody on a Theme of Paganini* and there's also a Bowie collection, *Liza Jane* and *Can't Help Thinking About Me* and *Never Let Me Down*. I pull one record out of its sleeve and it's unscratched.

I signal to my henchman that I'm taking the turntable with me to the hotel and that he is to carry the record collection.

"I'll come back with the ladies tomorrow," I say.

We still need kitchen fixtures and other furniture. Would they want a bookcase?

Bingo takes his role seriously and walks ahead of me, clutching the LP collection in his arms. He moves with slow, cautious steps to ensure his precious cargo doesn't stir. When we reach the hotel, I tell him he can put the box down. It has stopped raining and I notice a flowerpot has been installed by the entrance.

"I used to sing in a choir before the war," he says suddenly from where he is standing on the hotel steps. "Baritone."

May's words echo in my mind: "Every man has killed here."

"Yes, I used to sing in a choir myself," I say. That's actually where I met my wife—ex—in the choir.

I could have added: "I didn't really exist yet back then."

What if he answered: "And now? Do you exist now?"

206

The land that flows with milk and honey

Fifi has news. Good news.

"We've got our first bookings," he says. "Three, to be precise, though not until next month."

And that's not the only piece of good news because the archaeologists he was telling me about will be arriving in two weeks' time.

"They've confirmed. And reserved a room. So things are starting to move," he adds.

He stands by the computer in a semi-uniform: a white shirt and tie, but torn jeans and canvas sneakers.

"Just trying to look the part," he says to explain the tie.

He says one of May's friends in the house is going to take care of the cooking when they open the restaurant.

"My sister has organised it all."

To celebrate the news, May's friend is in the hotel kitchen as we speak, boiling beef that will soon be ready.

"It'll be a change from my pea soup," Fifi adds.

He turns the computer so that I can see the screen and says he's adjusting their website, which hasn't been updated since before the war.

"We emphasise the baths and the fact that all our rooms have their own character. How do you like it?"

"Nice."

He says there's something he'd like my opinion on. Since it is now clear that their aunt won't be coming back, he and

his sister have been thinking about changing the name of
the hotel. They have a few possible names in mind.

How do I like Blue Heavens Hotel? Or Hotel Blue Sky
Unlimited? Another possibility might be Paradise Lost Hotel.

"What do you think?"

"Isn't Hotel Silence just fine?"

There is a long pause.

"Yes, maybe we should stick to silence," he says, slipping
his headphones back over his ears.

With a shimmering sky on the eyelids

Twelve days have passed and the actress has returned.

I meet her on the stairs and I feel as if I'd stumbled on
a slightly electrified fence.

I observe her. She seems depressed and serious.

"How was the trip?" I ask.

"Everything is in ruins," she says. "The community's
entire infrastructure has been destroyed."

I've got a swollen cheekbone, bloodshot eyes, and a white
plaster over my eyebrow. She looks worried.

"I heard you were attacked," she says.

"Yes, somebody doesn't like me taking a vacation here."

"Are you okay?"

And she raises her hand, slowly, as if she were about to
touch the wound, but then just keeps it suspended in the air,

close to my face, as if she were about to stroke my cheek, but then just as suddenly allows it to sink again.

"It's nothing to be worried about," I say. "The guy who attacked me used to sing in a choir," I add.

She stares at me as if trying to solve a riddle.

"I also heard that you've been helping women. People talk."

"Yes, I'm helping them fix up a house."

She takes a deep breath.

"Every woman has lost someone, a husband, a father, a son, or brothers. Children have lost fathers or older brothers. Those who survived have lost arms, legs, or some other body parts."

"Did you find the locations for the documentary?"

"The women are cautious and don't want to talk about what they've been through. They don't want to be interviewed. They're tired. They're trying to understand what happened."

She pauses.

"Then a generation will grow up without any memory of it. Then there'll be the danger of a new war."

She falls silent.

"That won't be for another ten years yet, though," she adds, "because that's how long it takes to create a new generation of men."

Then she takes on a distant air and her voice changes, as if she were tired.

"Towards the end there were more mercenaries, some kind of private army working for security corporations. They directly participated in the attacks. People can't win a war without the involvement of private security services. They pay huge sums. They're the same companies that manufacture the weapons, produce the mercenaries, and work on the reconstruction after the war. Now these same entities are building drug companies and pharmacies everywhere. They ask if people have headaches and give them aspirin. They say that no one should have to feel pain."

"But the script?"

She doesn't answer the question, but says she's finished doing what she intended to do.

"I'm leaving tomorrow," she says, looking me straight in the eye. "So this is my last day."

She smiles.

At me.

The last day also means the last night.

"I'll come to you tonight," I say without any preamble.

A coat of flesh

I quickly glance in the mirror and run my hand through my hair before closing the door behind me.

Her room is number eleven, at the very bottom of the corridor.

She stands opposite me and pulls the bedspread off the bed, but doesn't fold it. Pigeons are cooing outside the window.

I unbutton the top button of my red shirt, peel back to the flesh. Under the shirt is a white water lily and under the water lily a heart still beats. Then I undo the next two buttons, while she handles her buttons and zips. Once I've taken off my shirt and trousers, I remove my socks, it doesn't take long. I take off my underpants and stand in front of her on the floor, stark naked. In the centre of the forest painting over the bed, between the black tree trunks, stands a hunter with a bow and arrow, who is looking a leopard in the eye. It is then that I notice that between the trees there is a winding path that seems to lead out of the painting. I stretch out my hand, grope towards her and take one step forward, there are still three floorboards between us. Then I take another step, a moment later skin touches skin. We press our palms against each other, lifeline against lifeline, artery against artery, I feel the pulsations through my entire body, my neck, knees, and arms, I feel the blood pumping between my organs. Then I touch her collarbone.

"Is that a flower?" she asks, placing her palm flat on my chest.

I take a breath. And then exhale.

STEEL LEGS LTD.

I phone Waterlily and get straight to the point, while Fifi fiddles with the computer.

"Doesn't . . ." I try to remember my daughter's ex-boyfriend's name. "Is Frosti still working in that prosthetics firm?"

I explain to her on the phone that I'm in touch with a physiotherapist who works on the rehabilitation of land mine victims. The physiotherapist is one of the women in the house who May introduced me to.

"Most of the people who lose a limb do so after a war," I say.

"I see."

"The woman I'm in touch with says she gets limbless people in a very bad state, but that they leave her walking on artificial legs."

I continue:

"I need prosthetic legs for fourteen people."

"Yeah?"

"For a seven-year-old boy, an eleven-year-old girl, a fourteen-year-old teenager, a twenty-one-year-old woman, and for a thirty-three-year-old and a forty-four-year-old man." I rattle off part of the list and tell her I'll be taking the measurements and sending them to her.

I hesitate:

"And I need to get a loan from you for this."

There is a silence at the other end of the line, then she says:

"Dad, aren't you coming home soon?"

"Not straightaway. You're visiting your granny, aren't you?" She lowers her voice and I get the feeling she's moving.

"I'm actually at granny's right now."

"Hang on," she says and I hear her raising her voice to explain something to her granny.

In the meantime, I wait and worry about the phone bill.

"Granny wants to have a word with you, Dad."

I hear her handing Mom the phone.

"Hello, this is Gudrún Stella Jónasdóttir Snæland."

"Yes, it's me, Mom."

"Waterlily tells me you've gone travelling. Are you abroad? Are you settling your affairs?"

"I suppose I am."

"What's the weather like? Isn't it always the same weather abroad?"

"It's raining."

"Is there a war?"

"No, the war is over."

"The guilty ones get away. It's always the innocent ones who suffer."

"Yes, I know, Mom."

"Your father and I went to the War Museum on our honeymoon, that's how romantic he was."

"Yes, you mentioned that."

Then she wants to remind me of the branch that beats against the window.

"You were going to saw it off for me. Don't you have your father's saw?"

I suddenly have an image of my mother dancing on the linoleum in the kitchen. She is wearing a dappled blouse and has slipped a record on the turntable and I stand there watching her. My arm is wrapped in a sling, home alone with Mom and not going to school for a few days. What record was she listening to? Little Richard? She wants to show me how to twist and grabs my unbroken arm. I'm in my socks.

Waterlily comes back on the phone.

"Do you think it's possible to love someone you've only seen?" she asks me.

"Why do you ask?"

"No, because I saw a man at the bank yesterday."

And then there's something else weighing on her heart.

"It occurred to me that we could go on a mountain walk when you come home. I bought hiking boots. I long to sleep in a tent for as many nights as possible this summer."

Then silence erupts, like a mountain

I notice Fifi occasionally glancing at me as I'm talking on the phone. When I've hung up, it's as if he's about to ask me something but then thinks better of it.

Instead he says:

"They came and took away the other guest last night."

"Who came? Took who?"

"The police. The man in room nine. He was led away in handcuffs."

"What happened?"

He tells me that Adam had slipped into the man's bedroom while May was cleaning and had hidden himself in a wardrobe. When he was found, they also found artefacts that had been bought on the black market—in addition to the three breasts that were missing from the mosaic—so they notified the police.

"He'll be charged with theft and the illegal sale of antiquities."

He then switches topics:

"We decided to follow your advice and keep the name Hotel Silence. And we put up a sign. In three languages." He points at a sign behind him.

"Silence saves the world," it says.

I count the steps between you and me

May opens the door, she is wearing a green buttoned cardigan.

"For you," I say, handing her the record player. "You just have to plug it in."

215

"You didn't need more time" is the first thing she says to me. "You just didn't want me."

I ask her if I can come in and she nods.

The boy is asleep in bed, with a gaping mouth and open palms. Beside him lies an alphabet book with pictures. She tells me that the school will be reopening in the autumn and that he has started to practice reading.

Once I've plugged in the turntable, I fetch the collection of records.

I pull *Ziggy Stardust* out of its sleeve and slip it on.

"I was wondering if you could teach me how to dance."

What was it that Mom said again? That when the racket of machine guns has stopped people feel a need to dance and go to the movies.

She looks at me with a grave expression for a moment, then bursts into a laugh.

I feel I need to explain myself.

"My wife—ex-wife—said I didn't know how to dance."

"What kind of dancing? You mean a two-step?"

"Just how a man dances with a woman."

It's a difficult thing for me to say.

"When do you want to start?"

"Right now? That's if you're not busy. If it doesn't wake Adam up."

She says:

"He was used to sleeping through air raids."

And then:

"You place one hand here and I hold you here, you step forward and I step back, then I step forward and you back."

We're standing in the middle of the tiled floor, bang in the centre, then we move towards the window.

"Picture this as a journey," she continues.

"Like this?"

"Yes, like that. It's like walking."

"We're alike, you and I," I say.

"I know," she says without looking at me.

She hesitates. Then:

"This morning I could smell grass again for the first time."

The light from the stars needs time

"There are some sunrises that stand out," Svanur had said. The sun rises. Slices the sky in two. Without shedding any blood. First there is a horizontal line of light along the floor, a single streak, then more and more streaks until a puddle of light forms on the floor.

I'm shaving when I'm called to the phone. Fifi is in his tracksuit trousers and looks like he's been woken up.

"She says she's your daughter," he says.

I immediately know something is wrong from the tone of her voice.

"It's Svanur, Dad. He walked into the sea. His dog was found on the beach, totally drenched. She'd swum after him but turned back."

"Does anyone ever recover from being born?" Svanur had asked. "If people were given a say," he added, "might they decide not to be born?"

She says she'd dropped by the apartment two days ago to water the plant and met Svanur outside.

"He was vacuuming the caravan and thought he'd heard some suspicious sound coming from my car as I was driving onto the street. He thought it might be the wheel alignment on the right-hand side and offered to check it out. Then he embraced me and said that woman is the future of mankind. I've been trying to find out if that's a quotation from somewhere."

17 JUNE

"Hey," says the cabdriver, when he throws the suitcase into the trunk and invites me to sit in the front. "I've driven you before. Not long after Mick Jagger. I said it to myself the second I saw you: It's him. The man with the toolbox."

NOTES

In a number of places in the book there are quotations from Jónas Thorbjarnarson's collection of poems *Hvar endar maður?*. In most cases—not all—these are chapter titles, occurring on pages 74, 76, 102, 104 and 122.

There are loose translations from Friedrich Nietzsche's *Thus Spoke Zarathustra* on pages 20, 21, 53, 77, and 177, as well as from *Beyond Good and Evil* on pages 31, 127, and 217.

Poems by Steinn Steinarr are quoted on pages 87 and 123. The quotation on page 107 is from the sculptor Jón Gunnar Árnason.

The heading on page 137 is an indirect reference to St. Paul's Letter to the Corinthians in the Bible, and page 139 quotes from the prophet Isaiah.

PUSHKIN PRESS

Pushkin Press was founded in 1997, and publishes novels, essays, memoirs, children's books—everything from timeless classics to the urgent and contemporary.

Our books represent exciting, high-quality writing from around the world: we publish some of the twentieth century's most widely acclaimed, brilliant authors such as Stefan Zweig, Marcel Aymé, Teffi, Antal Szerb, Gaito Gazdanov and Yasushi Inoue, as well as compelling and award-winning contemporary writers, including Andrés Neuman, Edith Pearlman, Eka Kurniawan, Ayelet Gundar-Goshen and Chigozie Obioma.

Pushkin Press publishes the world's best stories, to be read and read again. To discover more, visit www.pushkinpress.com.

THE SPECTRE OF ALEXANDER WOLF
GAITO GAZDANOV

'A mesmerising work of literature' Antony Beevor

SUMMER BEFORE THE DARK
VOLKER WEIDERMANN

'For such a slim book to convey with such poignancy the extinction of a generation of "Great Europeans" is a triumph' *Sunday Telegraph*

MESSAGES FROM A LOST WORLD
STEFAN ZWEIG

'At a time of monetary crisis and political disorder… Zweig's celebration of the brotherhood of peoples reminds us that there is another way' *The Nation*

THE EVENINGS
GERARD REVE

'Not only a masterpiece but a cornerstone manqué of modern European literature' Tim Parks, *Guardian*

BINOCULAR VISION
EDITH PEARLMAN

'A genius of the short story' Mark Lawson, *Guardian*

IN THE BEGINNING WAS THE SEA
TOMÁS GONZÁLEZ

'Smoothly intriguing narrative, with its touches of sinister,
Patricia Highsmith-like menace' *Irish Times*

BEWARE OF PITY
STEFAN ZWEIG

'Zweig's fictional masterpiece' *Guardian*

THE ENCOUNTER
PETRU POPESCU

'A book that suggests new ways of looking at the world
and our place within it' *Sunday Telegraph*

WAKE UP, SIR!
JONATHAN AMES

'The novel is extremely funny but it is also sad and
poignant, and almost incredibly clever' *Guardian*

THE WORLD OF YESTERDAY
STEFAN ZWEIG

'*The World of Yesterday* is one of the greatest memoirs of the twentieth
century, as perfect in its evocation of the world Zweig loved, as it is
in its portrayal of how that world was destroyed' David Hare

WAKING LIONS
AYELET GUNDAR-GOSHEN

'A literary thriller that is used as a vehicle to explore big
moral issues. I loved everything about it' *Daily Mail*

FOR A LITTLE WHILE
RICK BASS

'Bass is, hands down, a master of the short form, creating in a few pages
a natural world of mythic proportions' *New York Times Book Review*

JOURNEY BY MOONLIGHT
ANTAL SZERB

'Just divine… makes you imagine the author has had private access to your own soul' Nicholas Lezard, *Guardian*

BEFORE THE FEAST
SAŠA STANIŠIĆ

'Exceptional… cleverly done, and so mesmerising from the off… thought-provoking and energetic' *Big Issue*

A SIMPLE STORY
LEILA GUERRIERO

'An epic of noble proportions… [Guerriero] is a mistress of the telling phrase or the revealing detail' *Spectator*

FORTUNES OF FRANCE
ROBERT MERLE

1 *The Brethren*

2 *City of Wisdom and Blood*

3 *Heretic Dawn*

'Swashbuckling historical fiction' *Guardian*

TRAVELLER OF THE CENTURY
ANDRÉS NEUMAN

'A beautiful, accomplished novel: as ambitious as it is generous, as moving as it is smart' Juan Gabriel Vásquez, *Guardian*

A WORLD GONE MAD
ASTRID LINDGREN

'A remarkable portrait of domestic life in a country maintaining a fragile peace while war raged all around' *New Statesman*

MIRROR, SHOULDER, SIGNAL
DORTHE NORS

'Dorthe Nors is fantastic!' Junot Díaz

RED LOVE: THE STORY OF AN EAST GERMAN FAMILY
MAXIM LEO

'Beautiful and supremely touching… an unbearably poignant description of a world that no longer exists' *Sunday Telegraph*

THE BEAUTIFUL BUREAUCRAT
HELEN PHILLIPS

'Funny, sad, scary and beautiful. I love it' Ursula K. Le Guin

THE RABBIT BACK LITERATURE SOCIETY
PASI ILMARI JÄÄSKELÄINEN

'Wonderfully knotty… a very grown-up fantasy masquerading as quirky fable. Unexpected, thrilling and absurd' *Sunday Telegraph*

BEAUTY IS A WOUND
EKA KURNIAWAN

'An unforgettable all-encompassing epic' *Publishers Weekly*

BARCELONA SHADOWS
MARC PASTOR

'As gruesome as it is gripping… the writing is extraordinarily vivid… Highly recommended' *Independent*

MEMORIES—FROM MOSCOW TO THE BLACK SEA
TEFFI

'Wonderfully idiosyncratic, coolly heartfelt and memorable' William Boyd, *Sunday Times*

WHILE THE GODS WERE SLEEPING
ERWIN MORTIER

'A monumental, phenomenal book' *De Morgen*

BUTTERFLIES IN NOVEMBER
AUÐUR AVA ÓLAFSDÓTTIR

'A funny, moving and occasionally bizarre exploration of life's upheavals and reversals' *Financial Times*

BY BLOOD
ELLEN ULLMAN

'Delicious and intriguing' *Daily Telegraph*

THE LAST DAYS
LAURENT SEKSIK

'Mesmerising… Seksik's portrait of Zweig's final months is dignified and tender' *Financial Times*